The Sex Diaries

Lauren Spice

Published by Pettway Publishing, 2021.

THE SEX DIARIES

First edition. July 3, 2021.

ISBN: 979-8224417100

Written by Lauren Spice.

the SEX DIARIES

LAUREN SPICE

Chapter 1

Megan accepted the stack of journals, surprised at how heavy the notebooks could be. The pages were worn with writing on the front and back. She shifted the weight in her arms, a vain attempt to make them easier to hold.

"Thank you," Lori's weak voice said. "I never thought I would see these things be read by someone other than me." She smiled, her face trembling with the effort. "Thank you for accepting this project."

Megan nodded. "My pleasure."

But she felt uncomfortable around the sick woman. She took the journals and left the room. Lori had set up her resting spot on the sofa in the living room, so Megan moved to the dining room. She could hear Lori coughing occasionally, but at least, she didn't have to converse with her while she was trying to complete the job.

After barely eking out a living on some blogs and articles for the paper, this job offer paid well, and she wanted to focus one-hundred percent. Megan began to sort the journals by date. Taking a deep breath, she selected the first journal and noted that the two had met when they were nineteen, based on the dates.

She opened it and flipped through a couple of entries before she came to the one where Lori and Klayton met. Feeling like a snoop, Megan settled back into the dining room chair and began reading.

'The guy I met today is *so* cute. His name is Klayton, and he's a junior. He told me what he was studying, and it's something sciency. I totally forgot as soon as he said it.' Megan tried not to pass judgment on Lori, but she seemed a little airheaded. Who doesn't remember every detail about the cute guy they just met?

'He came over and talked to me which is a first. I'm normally the quiet girl that people ignore at parties, so when he came over and talked to me, I acted like a total idiot. I didn't know what to say. He was all like 'What's your name?' and I couldn't give him a straight answer. Why am I such a klutz around guys? He'll probably never speak to me again.'

Megan skimmed the part where she was agonizing over every detail of their conversation. She wondered if Klayton remembered their first conversation and made a note to interview him when he got home from work. He was the one who had hired her over the phone, but she had never actually met him. She tried to get a better picture of this junior in college who had gotten Lori's attention. Was he a jock? A nerd? A guy with one thousand friends?

Megan skipped a couple of days where Lori was just wondering if she would ever see him again and what she should do if she did. She stopped when she reached the point where Lori saw him again.

'He was there with his friends, and I thought he was purposely ignoring me at first. He was just laughing and joking with them. I was by myself, trying to study. Then, he saw me and came over. He actually came over! We talked for a couple of minutes. He asked me about my classes, then he tried to convince me to stop studying.' So he wasn't the nerd after all. Lori's picture of him was so generic that he could really be anyone. Brown hair and brown eyes. Could she get any more boring? But then again, that was why Megan was there she thought. To rewrite their story using more creative words.

She started reading again. 'He said I should live a little. And I never want to act like the party pooper. Plus, no other guys asked me out. This was my *one* chance. So, I said yes. Oh my gosh, I said I would go hang out with him. And I was thinking that was all it would be. No way. He and I went to his dorm room and hung out, but his roommate was gone.'

Megan sat up. She could see where this was going. Lori did not seem like the type to sleep with a guy she just met when she squealed about him like such a little girl in her journals.

'I remember every moment, and I don't want to forget any of it, in case it doesn't happen again. I was sitting on his bed, and he was getting something from his desk. He is so sexy from the back. I felt myself getting wet just thinking about what he would look like without clothes on. He turned around, and it was like he could read my thoughts. He offered me something to drink, but I don't do alcohol, so I said no. He promised me it wasn't alcohol, just juice. And he was right. It tasted normal. I don't know why I was considering sleeping with a guy if I didn't even trust what he was serving me to drink.' Megan skimmed some details about Klayton's room and that he seemed like a neat freak. Then, she got to the good stuff.

'Just laying next to him on the bed watching the movie was really distracting. I kept thinking little things like what he would do if I touched his stomach or his pants or his face. And then, my hand just reached out and touched him by itself. I tugged at his shirt and touched the skin underneath. I pulled back as soon as I did. I couldn't believe I just did that. But he didn't feel embarrassed at all. He rolled onto his side and kissed me. He kissed me hard. He pulled my lips into his mouth. I never felt like that when a guy kissed me before. It was like I just wanted him to kiss me forever. He started touching me through my pants, and I kept wondering in the back of my mind if his roommate was going to come in.

'Then, he took my hand and guided it inside his pants. I could feel him so hard. I didn't know that when they say 'a guy is hard' that they mean like *that* hard.' Megan looked up, realizing that Lori must have been a virgin when she met Klayton. Wow. This was going to be an interesting read. No longer feeling like she was reading a journal but more like some sort of romance story, Megan dove back into the dorm room.

'I wanted to see what was going on, but he kept kissing me. He didn't know he was my first, and it wasn't like I could tell him right then. I wanted to enjoy it, but I just kept wondering if he had a condom and if his roommate was going to come in. But when he started touching me, it was like I couldn't think about anything else. I don't know how he knew it would make me feel so good. But he just kept sliding his fingers back and forth. It felt weird, and part of me wanted to make him stop. But it felt good at the same time. I'm doing such a terrible job describing it. Anyway, before he got my pants off, his roommate did come in. He kind of laughed, and Klayton covered himself. Even though we didn't do it, I really wanted to. I think I would have let him too. I hope I get to see Klayton again.'

Megan heard a creak of the floorboard then footsteps. Looking up, she saw the man who must be Klayton standing in front of her. Did he know what part of the journal she had been reading?

"Klayton," she said, trying to sound as professional as possible. She rose to shake his hand, getting a real description of the man in the journal. Yes, he had brown hair and brown eyes, but he was so much more than that. He was clearly a man who enjoyed his time at the gym. His arm muscles were toned, and he filled out the T-shirt well. Megan glanced down for just a moment as their hands let go and replayed the scene she had read in the journal. Then, she smiled. This would be the perfect opportunity to get his perspective on what happened.

Chapter 2

"I've just been reading through the journals as you wanted me to do," Megan explained. "I thought I would be able to write a more thoroughly accurate story, however, if I got your perspective. I realize that the biography is focused on Lori, but I want to get the details correct."

"Sure, of course," Klayton said. "Let me put my bag away and check on Lori, and I'll come back in a minute to talk." He disappeared down the hall, and Megan had a few moments to organize her notes. She pulled out her laptop and opened a fresh document. It would be much easier to keep track of his answers there than on paper. It didn't hurt that he wouldn't be able to see what she was writing as she wrote it. She heard Klayton and Lori talking in the front room. She could hear the murmur of their voices but not what they were saying. Finally, Klayton re-entered the dining room.

"Thanks for waiting. I'm happy to answer any questions you might have."

"Sure, I've been reading from the beginning, and I read about when Lori met you. I just wanted to get that day from your perspective."

Klayton blinked his eyes a couple of times. "If I remember correctly, she was wearing jeans and a purple college pride sweatshirt. It was pretty cold, but I don't remember the exact day, sorry."

Megan was not impressed with his answer. Was *this* how he remembered his wife? A compilation of factual details? "What did you *think* when you saw her? What did you do?"

"*Oh*!" Klayton seemed to understand better what she wanted. "I remember thinking that she seemed really shy and unsure of herself. I wanted to talk to her, because I always feel bad for the lonely kid. So, once we talked, she seemed interesting. We talked about what we were studying and high school, stuff like that."

"And do you remember the next time you saw her?" Megan's stomach turned over in anticipation where she was leading Klayton.

He nodded. "Sure, the next time was a bit more memorable. I was getting a smoothie from one of the shops on campus, and she was studying there. I suggested she study in my room."

"What were your intentions with inviting her to your room?"

Klayton laughed. "You sound like her father."

Megan shrugged. "I'm just trying to get the details right."

Klayton set his chin in his hand and stared directly into Megan's eyes. She wanted to look away. How could she stare into his eyes as he explained a sexual encounter with his college girlfriend, now wife? Megan averted his gaze, focusing on the computer screen, even though she could type without looking.

"I thought that if we were studying in my room, that anything could happen. Studying in a café leaves zero opportunity." Megan's lips twitched as she wrote his answer. At least Klayton was upfront. She already knew a little bit about what type of guy he was based on the fact that he and Lori had slept together on their second date, if their encounters could even be called dates.

"She agreed to watch a movie instead of studying. We were laying on my bed, and let the record show that she touched me first."

Megan chuckled just a little.

"And?" Megan asked, waiting. This time, she didn't look away from the deep brown eyes staring at her. "And, we did what college kids do. We started touching. I let her feel me. And I could tell when she did that she had never been with a guy before. She was so 'oh' and 'wow.' So, I took it slow with her. We just touched."

Megan swallowed before asking him. "How did you touch?"

"I reached in her panties and moved my fingers to make her wet. She was practically pushing herself into my hands, and she was already wet. I wanted to go further, but I thought she might freak out since it was her first time. Better to do it in small doses, you know?"

"Were you planning to stay with her? I mean, my understanding is that you didn't have an official relationship at this point."

"No, we didn't. But I was definitely planning on keeping her around." Klayton blinked at Megan, but she was still thinking back on his last statement, about how he had wanted to make her feel good. Megan wondered what it would feel like to have him touch her.

"Is that your typical technique?" she asked with a raised eyebrow. Klayton shrugged, maintaining such strong eye contact that Megan couldn't keep her cheeks from reddening.

"I don't have a typical technique. I do what the woman wants." His eyes fell to Megan's breasts, and she wondered if he was as turned on by this conversation as she was. She lowered her voice just a little.

"What's your favorite sex position?" Megan asked with boldness.

Klayton bit his lower lip. Was he trying to turn her insides to jello on purpose? "I like to be on top," he said. "What about you?"

"I didn't know I was being interviewed," Megan said. Her fingers stopped their tapping on the keyboard. "But since you asked, I like when a guy is on top of me." They both just looked at each other for a minute. Megan could have stayed there forever, sending messages with her eyes. But Lori's bleating voice from down the hall called Klayton's name.

"Klayton, can you please look at my medicine tray? I think one of the pills is missing." The husband stood up, still making eye contact with Megan. He looked down at himself then at her again, and Megan noticed that he was hard. Then, he turned and walked out of the room to take care of his wife.

Megan turned to the journals. She had come here to complete a job, and that did not include touching the one who had hired her.

Chapter 3

The next day, Megan arrived at Lori and Klayton's house at one o'clock sharp. She was supposed to interview Lori to get any details she might have missed putting in her journals. Based on the depth of detail in the journals, Megan doubted that there was a lot she had missed.

"How are you feeling today?" Megan asked, setting up her laptop and getting ready to take notes.

"Not well," Lori said. Her voice was soft and raspy. Megan knew that she had cancer of the throat. It meant that she couldn't eat regular food but had to be fed through a pump. Other than that, she didn't know a lot of details. Nor did she want to know them. She hadn't become a nurse for a reason. She didn't enjoy anything involving bodily fluids.

"I'm sorry to hear that. Can I get you anything before we get started?" Lori shook her head.

"I wanted to ask you about when you first met Klayton. I read your journals, but you're missing some key details. Where were you when you met? What led up to your meeting him? Anything else that might help set the scene."

"It's not all about him," Lori rasped out. "You're supposed to be writing my biography, not just focusing on our relationship. You are including everything, aren't you?"

Megan cleared her throat while she made a note on her computer. 'Very demanding and wants to take charge.' She managed to force a smile on her face. "I am getting as much detail as I can in your story, but we also don't want to include a lot of extra details. Some of your early journal entries focus on just your day-to-day school life."

"Make sure you include when I went to the state championship for the writing contest. I didn't win anything, but I was the only student from my district to reach the championship. If it was up to me, you wouldn't be writing this at all, but I just don't have the energy I used to." Lori coughed, and her voice faded into a whisper. "Klayton wanted to hire someone to help me with it. He's very thoughtful that way."

Megan took a few more notes. 'Thinks she's a good writer. Proud of high school achievement. Life doesn't revolve around Klayton.'

"Any reason you two didn't have kids?" she asked.

Lori frowned. "That's personal."

Megan blinked for a few moments. She had read the intimate details of this woman's first sexual encounter, but Lori didn't want her to know about their reason for not having kids? Megan shrugged, now more interested than before. Maybe Klayton would tell her. If he didn't, the journals probably would. She had only read through two the day before. She still had six more to read.

"What would you say is the biggest accomplishment of your life?"

Lori thought for a few minutes. She still wasn't thirty, and she had been sick for over two years. She hadn't had a lot of time to do anything big.

"I would say that working as a teacher was very rewarding. I was a teacher for three years, before I had to stop due to getting sick. Some of the students friended me on social media. You should reach out to them. I bet they could contribute to my biography." Megan made a note of the students' names. She didn't know this job would include conducting various interviews. What she really wanted was to interview Klayton again. She kept replaying that moment when Klayton had stood and had a tent in his pants. He had wanted her to see, and why would he want that unless he wanted her? Megan swallowed and focused on the project at hand.

She spoke with Lori for an hour, until Lori was having trouble speaking even at a whisper. "Sure, I understand that your voice needs to rest. I'll be in the dining room reading the journals." Feeling generous, Megan said, "If you need anything, just know I'm there." There was nothing wrong with Lori's legs. She could take care of herself and walk around, but Megan had noticed that she seemed to enjoy having someone take care of her. Megan jumped when she entered the dining room and found Klayton there, typing away at his laptop.

"Oh, hi!" she said instead of the swear word that was at the tip of her lips. "I did not know you were here."

"I didn't want to interrupt your conversation," Klayton said. "I got home and have some projects to complete." He nodded at the chair across from him. "Join me." Megan pulled out journal number three in the series and flipped it open, pressing the pages down so they wouldn't flip closed.

"I have to say this has been the most interesting job I've ever had."

Klayton smiled. "Why's that?"

"More interesting material. Most of what I've written before were blog articles about crypto currency or copywriting for business about boring things like trash chutes or bicycle repair."

"Glad this is something to break up the monotony," Klayton said. He had stopped typing on his computer, and he was making eye contact with her again. Megan's mind replayed the moment where he had stood up the day before and indicated how turned on he was. Megan wondered if he was starting to get a little excited just talking to her.

Of course he wasn't! He was a devoted husband. He had been talking about the first time being with his wife. Of course that turned him on! It had nothing to do with her being in the room. Megan blinked. Klayton was still looking at her.

"You're getting to know so much about me. I want to know more about you," he said. "I think I should know about the person who's completing this job."

"I gave you my references on the phone, and I sent you the email with the samples I've done."

"I know about your writing," Klayton said. "I mean more about you, as a person."

"Okay," Megan said, smiling just a little. It had been a while since she had had a casual, flirtatious conversation with a guy, and she'd never had one of those with someone who was married.

"Are you currently dating anyone?" he asked.

Megan shook her head. "No, are you?" she teased.

Klayton looked thoughtful for a moment before laughing softly. "Nope, not at the moment. What do you like to do for fun?"

"I like to read about people's sex lives," Megan held up the journal.

"Then recreate them?" Klayton suggested, leaning closer. Megan felt warmth between her legs. If she had thought he was flirting before, she knew he was now. Lori must have heard Klayton's voice, because the tinny sound of a ringing bell sounded. When Lori's voice was too bad and she needed something, she would use the bell. Klayton left, and Megan hated that he was always going to take care of Lori. But really, that was what he was supposed to do. Flirting didn't hurt anyone, but she wanted to talk with Klayton some more. She would wait until Lori was sleeping, then they could continue their conversation.

Chapter 4

Klayton didn't come back for half an hour, and Megan tried to focus on her reading. She barely got through a few journal pages, though. She was too busy thinking about Klayton, skimming for the naughty parts in the journal then pretending it was her. She had already read through a year of Lori's journal when she got to an especially delicious scene. She read it slowly.

'Even though we've been together eleven months, being with Klayton never gets old. Last night, I just wanted it to never end. So glad he upgraded to an apartment now that he's a senior. Having his own room makes it so easy. I barely ever sleep in my dorm room anymore. Last night, I asked him to give me a massage. I was sore from helping Darla move. I took off my shirt and turned my back to him. His hands can work magic. I wasn't trying to make anything happen. I swear. But when he started touching my back, I started groaning like he was taking me to the brink of finishing.

'He massaged my back then spun me around. I can't believe he just put his hands in my underwear and pulled me against him. He was all like 'I need you.' And I told him that it didn't count as a massage if he stopped halfway through, and he said there were other ways to massage me.

'He pushed me forward and spread my legs, and sometimes, I really like it when he just takes over like that. I put one of my hands back on his hairy leg, and . . .'

Megan looked up when Klayton re-entered the room. She swallowed hard. She wanted him to do to her the same things he had done to Lori. She wanted to experience what she had just been reading about. Klayton smiled at her casually. He clearly had no idea what sort of scene she had just been reading.

"Lori's all settled now," he said.

"That's good. She seemed to be not feeling well. That was why we stopped our interview." Megan cleared her throat and took a deep breath. She could do this. She could fake normal conversation.

"What were you reading?" Klayton asked.

"Oh, I was . . . she was talking about you moving into the apartment, instead of the dorm." Megan fumbled with her words.

Klayton raised his eyebrows. He didn't believe her. He took the journal from the table and turned it around so he could see what she had been reading. Megan watched his face with a tightening in her legs. He looked up and smiled.

"You don't happen to need a massage, do you?" he asked. Megan forced herself to shake her head. How did he have such power over her? She was trying to pull on every thread of common sense that she had, but she couldn't stop him from rounding the table. His hands settled on her shoulders, two of his fingers sliding under the neck of her shirt. His skin was rough against her rounded shoulder muscles. He pressed his thumbs into her back, and her head fell forward, allowing him better access to massage. She wasn't doing anything wrong. He was the one touching her, she assured her conscience.

His hands squeezed her shoulders, then he pushed her forward and started kneading the muscles down the middle of her back. Megan stopped herself from groaning when he squeezed her arm muscles. She was telling herself that she should stand. She could turn around and tell him that she wasn't this kind of person. But before she could stand up, she felt his lips on her neck. He was kissing her neck gently, and it sent shivers up and down her back. His lips moved closer to her ear.

"Don't be afraid," he told her, three little words. He tugged at her shoulders, wanting her to stand up. She shouldn't, but her legs were already moving. She turned around and kissed him without thinking about it. He pulled her body against his, and she felt how hard he was. It took her a moment to realize what was happening, but when she did, she reached around him and slid her hands under his shirt, running her hands over his back and squeezing. He cupped her neck before separating their lips and continuing with a series of kisses down the side of her face and neck.

Megan took a deep breath, and they heard the shuffling of footsteps in the hall. Lori hardly ever got off the couch, but she was sure off now. Megan plopped back down into her chair and lowered her face to the computer, typing nonsense just to make her fingers look busy. Klayton grabbed the journal from the table and stood there reading it.

"Klayton," Lori said from the doorway, her voice switching from raspy to a whisper. "I didn't know you were home. Why didn't you say hello?"

Klayton smiled smoothly and pecked his wife on the cheek. "You two were interviewing when I came home, and I didn't want to interrupt." He pointed to something in the journal. "Hey, I didn't know …"

Lori snatched the journal out of his hand. "You're not supposed to read these. They're for Megan, not you." Megan continued to tap away on her computer as she listened to the nastiness in Lori's voice. Klayton didn't say anything mean back, though, as Lori thumped the journal back down on the table beside Megan.

"Klayton, come with me, I need help getting my feeding tube in." Klayton followed Lori, and Megan rolled her eyes after them. Lori clearly had a need to feel like she was in control. Megan flipped the journal back to where she had been reading and poised her fingers over the keyboard to take notes, but she was too distracted. She kept thinking about how it had felt to have Klayton touch her skin. When he had kissed her neck, she thought she would explode with desire. It was good they had stopped. She shouldn't be a home wrecker, but that didn't stop what she was feeling. Klayton didn't come back to the dining room for over an hour. So much for that work project he had to complete.

Megan left the house feeling like something was unfinished, and it wasn't just the biography. She was thinking about Klayton and wondering if she would see him the next day and if Lori would leave them alone long enough to really enjoy themselves.

Chapter 5

Megan had finished reading all but one journal, and she could see how even though Lori and Klayton had started out strong, the annoyances that filled day-to-day life had really distracted Lori once she got cancer and was too sick to have as much of a physical relationship.

When Lori answered the door that day, she looked exhausted.

"How are you feeling?" Megan asked as she always did. It felt rude not to acknowledge Lori's illness each day.

"I barely slept at all last night," Lori said. "It's exhausting hosting you every day to work on this project." Megan licked her lips trying to understand how Lori considered sitting in the living room and watching TV as hosting.

"Well, I'm working as hard as I can to complete the project in a timely fashion." She tried to keep her communication with Lori business-like.

"Good. I think once you finish reading the journals, you can just call us if you have more questions. You can work from your home."

Megan understood what Lori was saying. She was tired of having a stranger in her house and just wanted to be miserable alone. "Well, that should happen today," Megan said. "I should finish reading in a few hours."

"Good." Lori shuffled back to the couch and sat down. Megan made her way to the dining room. She picked up the last journal, but she couldn't focus. Lori was detailing a fight between herself and Klayton, and it wasn't as interesting as the reading about their early days. Megan paced around the dining room, holding the journal in front of her and trying to get through it. Really, she was wondering when Klayton was going to return from work. She didn't want to leave the house without saying goodbye, because it sounded like Lori really didn't want her ever coming back again.

Megan paced around the dining room again. She peered out of the dining room and down the hall. She could hear Lori coughing from the living room. She probably wasn't going to move for a while. Now would be Megan's chance. Feeling like a snoop, she looped through the dining room to the hallway that led to the guest bathroom and the master bedroom. There were pictures along the wall, and Megan had been meaning to look at them. If anyone caught her snooping, then she would say she was simply trying to understand more about the person she was describing.

Megan studied the pictures. It was easy to tell which pictures were young Lori and Klayton. Lori's skin looked perfect, no wrinkles or freckles, and she was always smiling at Klayton in the pictures instead of at the camera. In the later pictures, her eyes were harder, and she stared directly into the camera. Had something happened between the two of them or was it simply the natural parting that happens between some people?

Megan jumped when a hand touched her back. It was Klayton. Did he never work? He seemed to always be arriving home at the oddest of times.

"What are you doing back here?" he asked. His voice was low, and Megan took that as a cue to be quiet.

"Getting to know you a little better," she pointed to a casual picture on the wall where Klayton had his arm around someone who must be his best friend. The two guys were making silly faces at the camera.

"I've got a better way to do that," Klayton said, pushing her against the wall. "You really want to get to know me?" He had his hand on his belt buckle, and Megan nodded, entranced. Why was he so confident that Lori wouldn't come down the hall?

He slowly unbuckled his pants and slid them to the ground. Megan could see that he was hard already. He was wearing tight drawers that showed his form perfectly. Megan reached out and cupped his balls in her hand; everything seemed to be moving in slow motion, but Klayton sped things up. He reached for her pants and unbuttoned them with a practiced hand, slipping his hand under her underwear and moving his hand between her folds of skin. She moved closer, swinging her hips to help her pants fall a little further. She blinked at him. Was this really happening?

Then, she didn't have the chance to think anymore. Klayton's lips were on hers, and his desire for her made it barely possible to stop herself from putting him inside her right then and there. Megan stroked his sword, surprised at how warm he was. She felt how smooth the tip was, rubbing her thumb in slow circles over it. He pushed his hips into her, removing her hand from his underwear and pressing himself up against her, so she could feel how much he wanted her.

He was whispering in her ear. "I want to have you right now, but I'm going to make you wait." He laughed in a low tone.

Megan moaned, an odd combination of trying to control her desire and be quiet at the same time. Klayton squeezed her butt then pushed her against the wall and pulled her underwear to the ground. He squeezed her left breast as he nuzzled her neck. He was doing something with her other hand, but she couldn't see. Then, she knew, because he was free of his underwear and pressing just the tip of himself between her legs.

"You can do it all," she encouraged, wanting him to go inside her right then. She couldn't wait another minute.

"You can wait," Klayton said, his voice low in her ear. He kissed her long and slow, fondling her body as he did. Megan couldn't wait any longer. She stood on her tiptoes and held him to find his way inside her. The first push was slow and hurt just a little. Then, he pushed hard and fast, shoving her against the wall and making the pictures rattle. They had to be quiet, but it was hard to remember that as he touched her.

"I love it," she said. "Keep going, slowly." He slowed down, building the warmth inside her.

"I don't like slow," he whispered.

Pulling back, he spun Megan around like a practiced matador and repositioned himself behind her with a casual swiftness. Pushing himself back inside her, his first stroke was hard and deep.

"Oh God," Megan moaned.

His thrusts became harder, varying in depth. Megan could barely stand and her legs began to tremble. The sound of his pelvis slapping against her ass became as much of a turn on as the feeling of him inside her.

Klayton placed his rough hands on her trapezius muscles, squeezing and pulling her toward himself with every thrust. Megan felt as if she were in flight. With his right hand, he grabbed her hair and went so deep inside her that she yelped.

Putting his left hand over her mouth, he squelched her screams as they both came.

They both stood there, attached, as he slowly moved his hand from her mouth.

"I should, get dressed," Megan whispered.

"Megan," Klayton held her back for just a moment. "This thing between us, we should never pretend it didn't happen, and I want it to happen again." Megan smiled and dipped her head in acknowledgment. What could she say? It wasn't like her journalism degree prepared her for this.

She went into the bathroom and straightened herself, smoothing down her shirt and trying to pretend that nothing had happened. But as she looked in the mirror, she couldn't deny the silly smile that kept popping onto her face. She wanted more. She didn't want this to be the last time she saw Klayton. She had no idea what she would be facing when she left the bathroom, but she knew that Lori wouldn't be around much longer. And when she was gone, Klayton would need someone to keep him company.

Megan took a deep breath and stepped outside. Klayton wasn't there anymore, and a little part of her deflated. But what did she expect? They couldn't be lovers, at least not right now. He had duties. Megan went back to the dining room and sat at the chair in front of her computer. Smiling just a little, she poised her fingers over the keyboard and began writing her story with Klayton. She didn't leave out any details.

SHE LIKED TO WATCH

GILLIAN BLACK

Chapter 1

Elena dropped to her knees and began to scrub the floor. Before she'd come to America, she'd had so many dreams of success. Upon arrival, though, she'd learned that both of her advanced Mexican college degrees were worthless. She was a historian, by trade, but no one would even grant her a job interview. Her thick Spanish accent immediately made most people stereotype her and things were only getting worse. In the current political climate, people sometimes yelled at her to "Go back to Mexico!" or revved their car engines as she hurried across crosswalks and parking lots. The America of her dreams had all but disappeared. Now, she felt as though she had been set adrift in hostile territory.

That said, there were still bills to be paid. In fact, she was still paying off her immigration attorney and needed to send money back to her mother and younger sister. Back home, her family owned a small hotel with a restaurant attached on the first floor. Their establishment was popular with the tourists, but local gangs took huge cuts of their profits. Bribes had to be paid to local authorities to keep their license current, and since everyone knew that their establishment was doing a lot of business, these shady characters asked for a lot of money. They had no choice but to pay-up.

Recently, the roof had started to cave in, and so someone had to make the money needed for repairs since their Mexican insurance company had denied their claim on the ironic grounds that they'd accepted too high a percentage of American tourists that year. It seemed like everyone in the whole damned world was prejudiced against someone else and Elena was sick of it. Why couldn't everyone just get along?

So here she was, a woman with two degrees that had become just another living stereotype, feeling ashamed of herself because of that. So many years of her life had been spent in the library, thumbing through dusty books, learning about the histories and cultures of other lands, and yet here she was—on her knees scrubbing a rich man's floor, as though she'd never even picked up a history book. Granted, Elena didn't think any less of her housekeeping counterparts that weren't as educated, but she didn't feel like a part of their sorority, that much was certain. They had very little in common.

As a child, Elena had spent endless hours with her grandmother in the kitchen, mastering family recipes. In America, her knowledge of world history was not as useful as her ability to cook and clean. "Equal opportunity my ass," Elena muttered as she cleaned. She often talked to herself as she worked.

As she scrubbed the floor in wide circles, she thought about an image from one of her favorite history books. It was a photo in which Che Guevara, the Argentine military leader (and Marxist) was helping a young woman to her feet. Some historians had argued that right before the photo had been taken, the woman had slipped and Che had been simply offering a helping hand, yet Elena knew better. With Che, everything had been perfectly timed and calculated. The photo had been released by his strategist PR team of young dissidents, and it was intended to encourage the males inside Argentina to help their female counterparts to rise and take their place in the world—the photo was intended to wake up certain feminist ideals within society.

It was good PR—Che wanted people to know that he was hip to the times. "Look at me Mr. Jangles," Elena said to the dog licking his paws nearby. "Look at how I've moved up in the world." She added in Spanish. The dog's eyes seemed to laugh at her. Just then, one of her employer's many girlfriends entered the room. Elena could hear the harsh clacking of her shoes against the hardwood floor and the scent of her expensive perfume before she even turned around. Mr. Gale's latest girlfriend didn't know it yet, but she was expendable; they all were. Mr. Gale didn't keep any of his girlfriends for very long, especially the blondes. Elena had wondered why for a few months, but had eventually chalked it up to some kind of unresolved Oedipal complex. He loved women that reminded him of his mother, and then he also punished them for it. Elena' wiped some sweat off her forehead with the back of her hand. Sweat dripped down between her round breasts and perfect thighs. Elena's ass loomed high in the air as she crawled around on the floor, scrubbing.

"Elena, have you taken my clothes to the cleaners yet?" The latest blonde asked. She was Mr. Gale's newest flame, and her eyes were ice cold. Elena couldn't understand why anyone would want a girlfriend with crazy eyes like that. One eye went left and the other one went right. It was like her eyes were trying to bolt out of her head. This specific woman was mean as hell.

"Yes, Maam, I took your clothes to be laundered last night. Your dress for the party is supposed to be ready at one o'clock today." Elena finished. "Then, I expect you to have it back here and ready for me to wear by 1: 15pm. You know how Mr. Gale hates tardiness," the blonde finished. Elena lowered her head, silently hoping that the terrible woman wouldn't make any more requests of her today. "If it weren't for my yoga classes, I'd just be so stressed out all the time dealing with you people," the woman continued." You make my life so difficult," she said to Elena. "I bet you can't even read and write," the blonde whined. Elena lowered her head and said nothing.

"You do have a lovely figure, though, if I must say so myself. Are you fucking my boyfriend?" The blonde asked. " Of course, not, Miss." The fear in Elena's voice was audible. " Don't say *of course not*, like that would be above you people. You better not touch my man, because if I ever have any trouble out of you, you'll be on a plane back to Mexico before you can even say tortilla. My brother is an immigration attorney."

Mr. Jangles walked over and sniffed the woman's high heel. Out of nowhere, she kicked the small dog who yelped and limped backward, injured. Elena jumped to her feet. "Come on Mr. Jangles," Elena said as she lovingly scooped the pup up into her arms. She carried him back into the laundry room with her.

Mr. Jangles, didn't seem injured, but certainly wasn't in a very good mood now. She reached into a cabinet and handed the pup a treat. Elena scratched the top of his head while he gnawed on dog-cookie. "After I finish paying for my roof, you can come back to Mexico with me." She smiled. Mr. Jangles wagged his tale as if he was excited by that prospect. " You and I can run away together. We have birds for you to chase and chickens and lots of little brown fingers for you to bite!" Elena said playfully with a growl. This time when she reached for Mr. Jangles, he bolted (thinking she was trying to steal his beloved treat). The little dog knocked into a small cabinet that Elena had never noticed before. A small USB disk landed on the floor marked "Naughty Anna."

Elena picked the disk up and turned it over in the soft palm of her hand. She knew that she should mind her own business, but scrubbing floors was dull. She wanted to find out who Naughty Anna was. She'd just take a little peek, and then put the USB back into its spot in the cabinet. No one would ever need to know.

Chapter 2

When Elena popped the end of the disk into Mr. Gale's computer. She'd expected something boring, maybe footage of a golf game or Caribbean vacation, but what flashed across the screen was terrible. She immediately thought she was watching some kind of hostage home-movie.

A leggy blonde sat bound and gagged in a chair, with tears streaming down her face as she looked into the camera. Her mascara had run all the way down her cheeks, and her hair looked like it hadn't been combed in ages. She groaned in pain as she struggled to get out of the chair that she was tied to.

Elena brought both hands up to her mouth and gasped, terrified.

"What did I tell you never to do?" Mr. Gale's voice asked. The woman whimpered as she pulled at the restraints which bound her at the wrists and ankles. There was so much black mascara running all over her face that Elena could hardly make out of the woman's features. Had she seen her on a missing person's poster somewhere? The woman looked so familiar.

"Come on sweetheart, what did I tell you never to do?" The woman whimpered again. Was Mr. Gale some kind of serial killer?

Now, the camera was panning down her body. Her breasts were two perfectly rounded globes and a stream of sweat collected in the middle of her chest. "You look like you've been such a bad girl," Mr. Gale's voice crooned.

Mr. Gale started to stroke the woman's head as though she were some kind of pitiful dying animal. After a while, he pulled away the piece of cloth which ran between her huge botoxed lips and she gasped for air.

"I'm sorry, Sam." The woman blurted out. Mr. Gale laughed. "You're not sorry yet. You don't even know what sorry is, you little bitch." His voice was so sadistic. He pulled out a knife. " Sam!" The woman screamed. "Oh, come on, don't act like you don't like it—you know the safe word," he said. Elena raised an eyebrow.

Elena felt as though she might throw up. All this time she'd been cohabitating with some kind of maniac. Mr. Gale dragged the blade threateningly up and down the woman's thigh. When he pressed down, something unexpected happened. "Oh god, yes," the woman said, breathing heavily. Her breasts heaved as she gasped for air. "You're making me so wet," she exclaimed.

Elena's jaw dropped open.

Mr. Gale placed the camera down and started to untie the young woman. "This is what you said you wanted. Were you lying to me when you said you needed me to torture you?" Mr. Gale's voice asked. "No," the woman answered, shaking her head desperately. "If I find out you've lied to me, you realize how serious the consequences will be for you, don't you?" He continued. The blonde nodded again. " I want you to punish me. I deserve it." The woman spoke in a desperate voice.

Just then, Elena heard the automatic garage door opener. She slammed down the lid of the computer right before Mr. Gale sauntered into the room. He strode into the kitchen area wearing a pair of black penny loafers, carrying a dry-cleaned suit still beneath its plastic, swung nonchalantly over his back. He bent to his knees, and Mr. Jangles rushed over and started to lick his fingers eagerly. "Hi Elena," Mr. Gale said without even looking up. Elena looked over at Mr. Gale and then back over to the computer. She yanked the USB out of the port and hid it beneath the folds of her apron. "Hello, sir. I prepared a light snack for you this evening so that you might put something on your stomach before the banquet tonight," Elena said, rushing over to the oven.

Then, she gave him a huge smile. "Is everything okay?" Mr. Gale asked. "Oh yes, most certainly, sir," Elena said. Maybe she was overdoing it.

"The food smells great," Mr. Gale commented. He draped his suit across the back of the chair and sat down, while Elena placed a warm plate in front of him. A small sampling of all his favorite foods were there. She'd made him a mini quesadilla, two fried chicken wings, and a dollop of mashed potatoes with salsa and a sprinkling of cheese on top. Elena watched him out the corner of her eye as he ate. How could someone so beautiful lead such a terrible secret life? His curly blonde hair seemed to defy gravity as it reached skyward and his full pink lips seemed to pucker as he relished every bite of her cooking. "Mmmm.." he sighed as he chewed. The sound sent a spark of desire shooting through Elena's core, and so she smoothed her apron in order to push it away.

What a gorgeous serial killer, Elena thought. Too bad. What a waste. Hopefully, if he decided to kill her, it would be after payday.

As if reading her mind, Mr. Gale reached into his pocket and pulled out a huge wad of cash. "You've been so amazing these last few weeks," he said. "I want you to have this as a bonus," he said, his mouth still full of food. Elena felt a little strange about taking the money. Did he really mean it, or maybe he was going to be like the old lady down the street? She'd given Elena a bag of antique jewelry and then called the police, claiming theft. She'd almost been deported because of that mess.

Nevertheless, Elena couldn't afford to turn him down. "Thank you, sir," Elena said as she picked up the money and placed it inside her pocket.

"I'm planning a large dinner party next Friday. If I pay for all the supplies, would you cook for everyone? Your food is so delicious." Mr. Gale said. Of course, her food was amazing—her family owned a restaurant. Mr. Gale would know that if he'd ever bothered to ask her about herself. Immediately, though, Elena felt guilty for judging him so harshly. She'd never asked him about his family either, truth be told. While Mr. Gale addressed her with a great deal of professionality, he'd never hit her or tried to take advantage of her—which was more than could be said about her last employer's family. Yet, had she really sunk so low on the totem pole that the measure of a good man had simply become one who didn't beat her or try and take advantage of her in her sleep? Elena caught a glimpse of herself in the mirror across the room. She looked a lot like her grandmother—wearing all her housekeeping regalia. She had to make sure that her family could afford repairs on their hotel and restaurant—that was the only way to save the next generation. That was the only way to make sure this job was only a temporary gig.

Chapter 3

Elena rushed around the kitchen, preparing elaborate dishes on small plates. All of Mr. Gale's friends and family were there, and there was supposed to be a big announcement later in the evening. He wanted everything to be perfect. As a result, Elena had tweaked a few of her grandmother's recipes, and the gringos were eating her food up like it was going out of style.

Mr. Gale had asked her to buy 100 bottles of fine champagne, and Elena had spent over $30,000 on the gold-labeled bottles. The other staff members rushed in and out of the kitchen, as Elena rushed back and forth from the pots to Mr. Gale's massive industrial ovens. The kitchen was swelteringly hot, but for a moment she'd forgotten where she was. It was like being back in Mexico, working in her family's restaurant during the busy season. Elena loaded a tray with some small shrimp appetizers and then heard a voice call her out into the dining room.

"Elena, come out here!" Mr. Gale's voice called. Elena wiped her hands on a nearby towel and rushed out.

When Sam Gale had first seen Elena Dando, he had noticed that she was beautiful. Her dark hair was swept back in a messy bun, which somehow accentuated her large brown almond shaped eyes. He hoped that working for him hadn't been too distasteful. "Damien, this is Ms. Elena Dando—my executive chef."

Elena was surprised at the way Mr. Gale had chosen to introduce her. Executive chef? Was he out of his mind? Perhaps all that time torturing women had rotted his brain. Maybe he was just making a joke at her expense. Damien's eyes were serious as he took her hand and gently kissed the back of it—his lips lingering a few seconds too long. Mr. Gale noticed. "Let's not scare her away," Mr. Gale added with a smile. He then started talking about how she was a life-saver, how she'd brought life back to his household with her delicious food. "I own the Mexican gourmet restaurant downtown," Damien said. "Your food is better that what we serve. Would you consider a position with us?" Damien asked. Elene looked over at Mr. Gale for his approval—he only smiled. "Perhaps between functions for Mr. Gale, I might be able to find the time to help you, it would be my pleasure." Elena smiled. Then a slinky blonde woman sashayed over and looped her arm through Mr. Gale's arm. It was the woman from the video! So...she's not dead, Elena thought. "Sam, if we're going to make our plane, I think it's time." The woman smiled. "Right," Sam cleared his throat and tapped his champagne glass. The room froze.

"As many of you know, Anissa and I have been dating on and off for quite a while. I've never been one for monogamy, and I've always been a sucker for a pretty woman," the crowd laughed as Mr. Gale continued. He winked in the direction of the other blonde he was dating—the nasty one who'd kicked Mr. Jangles. "While Laura has been a great and beloved friend to me, Anissa has been kind enough to overlook my endless idiosyncrasies and has somehow stolen my heart. I've gathered all of you here today because I want you to know that I've asked Anissa to be my wife." He looked directly into Elena's eyes when he said the word 'wife.'

The room erupted in cheers and shouts of joy. Sam Gale leaned over and kissed Anissa hard on the lips, while his other blonde girlfriend, Laura, fled the room in tears. *That's what you get for kicking Mr. Jangles,* Elena thought to herself.

Yet, for some reason, Elena's own heart also suddenly dropped in her chest. There was something about the notion of Mr. Gale and Anissa together that seemed wrong, and suddenly she felt unsteady on her feet. There was something going on that wasn't quite right. Something in the scene unsettled her.

The next morning, Elena woke up early. She'd forgotten that she still had Sam's USB disk in her pocket, and it slipped out of her apron and clattered onto the floor as she got dressed. Elena picked it up, and examined both sides of the disk. Then, without much thought, she popped it into her own computer.

Again, the image of the leggy blonde, popped up on the screen, but there was much more to the video that Elena hadn't seen yet. "What do you think we should do with her, Anissa?" Mr. Gale asked in a mean voice. The other blonde woman walked over and kissed Laura slowly on the lips. Then, she withdrew and cupped the woman's breasts alternately.

They were having a threesome.

Sam took a deep sigh and set the camera down on some kind of nearby surface. He walked over to the two women, obviously incredibly aroused by the entire ordeal. Elena could see the outline of Sam's erect penis standing up straight inside his pants. He started to stroke Anissa's hair as she licked the side of the other woman's face. Then, he unbuttoned the clasp on his belt and allowed his pants to fall freely to the floor. Sam reached down and squeezed his crotch. Elena was ashamed to admit that the video was turning her on. Yet, Sam was undeniably handsome, and the sight of him with the two women made her wish he could touch her so tenderly.

Anissa dropped to her knees and began to nibble all along the outside of Sam's underwear. He gasped quietly. Then, she slowly pushed his underwear down, revealing his massive rod, which sprung out of his underwear, rock-hard. "Show me how much you like playing with me," Sam said. Anissa obediently took the throbbing head of his cock into her small mouth. It was evident to Elena that the woman was struggling with his girth. Then, Anissa began to suck as Sam bucked and thrust deep into her throat. Sam was merciless, and Elena couldn't help but think of how good it would probably feel to have him thrust into her womanhood that way. Yet, Sam was a wealthy man—a wealthy white man. It was unlikely he'd ever really take notice of her.

Chapter 4

Later that evening, after all the floors and counters had been scrubbed, Elena's curiosity got the best of her. What if that wasn't the only USB? What if there were more of them, more home movies? She looked around furtively and then headed for the cabinet in the laundry room. Elena had been right. There were more USBs—there were hundreds of them. She grabbed a handful and retreated to her room in the maids' quarters.

When Elena popped the next USB into her computer, she couldn't help but smile. It was a video of Sam's college graduation party. He stood there in his cap and gown, smiling into the camera—looking marvelously attractive and vibrant. "What are you going to do now, baby boy?" A male voice asked, off the screen. "I'm going to rule the world, of course," Sam answered with a giggle. Then, a line of static zagged across the screen. Maybe this was his graduation trip. Now, there was a petite brunette laying in the middle of a hotel bed, and Sam was behind her, thrusting into her pussy, doggy style, as if his very life depended on it. The woman moaned in pleasure, as Sam reached forward and grabbed a fistful of her hair, forcing her to lean backward and to tighten on instinct. "That's exactly what I like," Sam laughed as he continued to fuck her. Then, he withdrew and pumped his cock quickly as he slapped it against her face. A few minutes later he spewed his sticky white cum into the small cavern of her mouth. Sam pinched her nose shut and laughed as she swallowed his juices.

The video paused for a moment and then seamlessly segued into a shot of Sam at grad school—at around age 24. He had a whip in his hand and was standing there nude, as a girl with very long hair sucked his cock. Each time she came up for air, he cracked the whip along her bare back. The woman seemed to be near tears, but also seemed to be enjoying herself. "Take me all the way in," Sam said, as he pushed the woman's head down on top of his member. He groaned and bucked his hips for a little while. Elena thought he was going to cum again but was surprised to find that he rapidly withdrew and then threw the woman on the bed. Sam parted her legs and spat upon his cock, making himself wet. Then, he thrust himself into her asshole like some kind of wild animal. The woman cried out from both pain and pleasure, and Elena slammed the lid of her computer down.

He was a monster...well, maybe not a monster. Maybe he just had a high sex-drive. Maybe he just liked to fuck. Elena remembered the first time she'd caught her brother with her best friend, Nina. Sex was just a part of life, and all of these women had clearly consented. Just then, she heard someone called her name.

Elena stood and brushed off her outfit. Sam was standing in the foyer with two different ties, one in each hand. "Which one?" He asked. Elena slowly walked down the steps and pointed to the one on the left. "The yellow one brings out your eyes," she said. "Can you help me? I'm ashamed to admit that I never learned to properly tie these things," Sam continued. Elena gently took the tie from his hand. It was alarming to be so close to him. She noticed that her heart raced as she draped the fabric around his neck and leaned up on her tiptoes. Sam didn't back away. His face was incredibly close to hers, and he smiled and looked deeply into her eyes for a little while. "Your eyes look exactly like Kona beans," he said. "Excuse me?" Elena asked. "My favorite kind of coffee," he elaborated. "Coffee is Columbian, not Mexican," Elena answered smartly. "Well, Kona is actually Hawaiian—it's some of the finest coffee known to man. Bitter enough to be interesting, but sweet enough to feel smooth." Sam said. "Do you think I look Hawaiian?" Elena asked, trying to be playful. "I think you look beautiful," Sam said in a whisper which sent shivers racing up her spine.

Just then, Anissa noisily entered the room. She possessively looped her arm around Sam's elbow. "Get my bag, Elena," Anissa demanded. Her tone was so harsh that even Sam's face reddened. Elena and Sam had somehow managed to almost be equals for a few moments, but they lived in different worlds. His world would never accept her, and her world would never accept him—it was just the way things were.

Elena obediently grabbed Anissa's heavy leather handbag and held the door open for the two of them as they made their way out for a night on the town. "Have a good evening," Elena said sweetly to the couple. Anissa turned back with a sneer on her face, "don't forget to change all the linens in the guest rooms while we're gone. We're expecting Sam's parents in a few days. And try not to leave your dirty fingerprints all over my things this time Maria. I mean, Elena. if any of my things go missing, I hope you realize that I won't hesitate to call the police."

It was a veiled threat, but a threat nonetheless. "Yes, Ma'am," Elena said as she closed to door behind them.

For a moment, she feared that she might cry. It would be so easy for Anissa to call the police with some kind of made-up story about a missing wad of cash or piece of jewelry. Just one phone call could ruin her entire life, and her family needed the new roof. They needed it so badly that it wasn't worth the risk. She would have to stop thinking about Sam. She'd have to stop lusting after him and put him entirely out of her mind for good. Elena reached down to her pocket and fingered the USB disks that were still tucked away in her clothing. She needed to put them back.

Elena walked across the hall to the laundry room and dropped to her knees. She scooped all the USBs out of her pocket and prepared to put them back into their hiding place when someone coughed over her. Elena looked up. Sam was standing there with a bloody handkerchief up to his nose, having some kind of terrible nosebleed. "Good stuff, isn't it?" He said, as Elena clambered to her feet to help. She slammed the cabinet door and ran into the kitchen for some ice. Sam followed her at a slow pace.

Elena scooped a bunch of ice into a plastic bag while Sam tilted his head back. Then Elena gently plopped the ice-bag on the bridge of his nose. Sam winced. "Oh, don't be a baby," Elena said. "This is nothing compared to what you like to do to your girlfriends," she whispered softly.

" Tell me, Elena. Have you enjoyed watching my videos? Do you like my home movies?" Sam asked her in the sweet voice he'd used with Anissa. Then, he did something unexpected. He reached up and very gently began to finger the fabric of her dress. Elena moaned softly has his hands started to wander. He touched her waist and very slowly pulled her onto his lap where he moaned again softly. Then, very slowly his hands wandered up to cup her breasts. Elena felt as though she might orgasm right then and there. His touch sent chills up her spine, and she could feel his hardness swelling beneath her thighs. Sam wrapped his arms around her waist and pulled her into him even more tightly, before he started to grin against her body. Now Elena couldn't help but moan. She'd pictured this very moment so many times, and finally, finally his hardness was right there, hungry for her, aching for her perfect body. Elena reached down and cupped Sam's cock; she gave it a slight squeeze, through the fabric of his pants; he sighed.

Then, the door in front of them slammed, and the last thing Elena saw was Anissa, as she pitched her enormous leather handbag right at her head.

Chapter 5

When Elena woke up, she was surprised to find that she was in some kind of moving vehicle. Apparently, Anissa had thrown her handbag at her head so hard that it had knocked her out. There was a deep gash on her forehead, and Sam was holding tightly to her hand in the back of an ambulance. Elena could tell that he hadn't noticed that she was awake yet, and so she decided to enjoy the moment a bit longer.

Sam reached down and clicked on his cell phone. "You tell Anissa that I want her out by the end of the day. Consensual violence is one thing, but acting like some kind of crazed lunatic in my home will not be tolerated. I want her out. I'm done, do you understand? Done." Then, he was on the phone trying to coordinate medical care for Elena. "My lunatic girlfriend bashed Elena in the head!" Elena heard Sam growl. Then, unconsciousness took hold of her again, and she drifted into a dreamless sleep.

When Elena woke up, Sam was sitting at the foot of her hospital bed, looking pained. "I am so so sorry," he said as he kissed the back of her hand repeatedly "I want you to know that she's gone. Anissa and I are done." Elena reached up and felt a few bandages on her head. "Don't try and move," Sam said. "The saddlebag cracked your skull, and you had to have surgery to release the pressure. You've been out for three days." "Three days!" Elena was shocked. Then, worry took hold. She was certain that no one had called her mother. What had her family done? She was supposed to have sent them money for a payment for the roof two days ago. Elena tried to sit up, but Sam pushed her back down in the bed. "Don't try to move," he said. "The doctor says you shouldn't be up on your feet." Elena swallowed. "I have to send money to my family," she said groggily, "the roof. You don't understand; it's the only thing we have." Sam squeezed her hand. "I took care of all that already."

Elena's heart dropped in her chest. "What do you mean?" She asked. "I paid for the roof in full yesterday." He said softly. Elena felt both angry and moved all at once. Who did he think he was? Why did he have to be such a knight in shining armor? Even worse, did she look like someone that needed to be saved? How did he even know about the roof?

She felt violated and grateful all at once. Sam reached up and very gently stroked her hair back from her face. "Can I tell you something?" He asked her very softly. "I've been in love with you since the first moment I saw you," Sam whispered. A slight smile crept across his face. Elena paused for a long while. "That wasn't exactly the reaction I was hoping for," he said after a while. "Did you murder any of those women on the tapes?" Elena asked, after a while. Sam burst out laughing. "Of course, not," he said. Elena paused. "I had to ask. In this day and age, you never really know."

"The doctor says that you'll be ready to go home in a few days," Sam said trying to brighten the mood. "Am I being sent back to Mexico, for being involved in the altercation with Ms. Anissa?" Elena asked. Sam shook his head no. "How many years will I need to work for you in order to pay off what my family owes you for the roof?" Elena asked. Tears slowly started to roll down Sam's face. "You don't owe me anything," he said. You don't owe me a damned thing. "Then, he leaned down and kissed her soft lips.

Sam knew that what he was doing was probably wrong, but he couldn't help himself. She felt amazing. Even after being in the hospital for days, Elena somehow still managed to smell like fresh linen. She looked like a model, minus her black eyes. He reached down and pushed her hospital smock up. "Is this okay?" Sam asked. Elena nodded yes. Then, wordlessly he parted her legs with one large muscular hand. Very gently, he worked his way up to the pink nob which sat erect between her legs. He parted her legs and lowered himself on top of her and began to suck. Elena leaned back and moaned in deep satisfaction. Sam wasn't done. He pressed his fingers against her slit and entered her slowly as she lay there gasping. "Do you like me, Elena?" Sam asked sweetly, as he pumped his hand in and out of her sopping wet pussy. Elena nodded. "Then, maybe we can work out some kind of new arrangement? Maybe you can let me make you happy." He added.

Chapter 6

At the end of the week, Elena was cleared to go home. Sam had spent the entire time by her side in her hospital room, and when the nurses weren't nearby, he had so often pushed her hospital gown all the way up and sucked on her erect pink nipples. As she lay in the hospital bed, his hands repeatedly wandered between her shapely legs as he fingered her pussy and teased her clit. Elena was so horny for him that she felt she might go insane. His hand fit so perfectly inside her body. She couldn't wait to feel his hard rod inside her, thrusting and pounding her.

Most of the staff had commented on how attentive Sam had been, but little did they know the truth of what was happening behind closed doors. When Elena's dinner tray had been delivered at night, Sam had told her that she needed to earn her right to eat. He'd gently stroked her cheek as he pulled his massive cock out and offered it to her. Elena had gladly taken the hard member between her full lips and had sucked him hard, until he spewed far into the back of her throat. Then, he'd fed her a Salisbury steak, bite by bite, as though they were some kind of elderly couple.

Elena loved the game that had developed between them.

When they reached Sam's estate, she was surprised when he carried her inside. All of her belongings had been moved into the guest suite. She would no longer be required to clean, or to do anything except act as Sam's companion. Days turned into weeks, and weeks into months. Somehow, Elena's things made their way out of the guesthouse and into Sam's bedroom. Somehow the sexual games they played, opened their hearts. Both of them saw no one else and only had eyes for each other.

One night, when Sam was thrusting his manhood into the tight canal of her pussy three words slipped out of his mouth. "I love you," Sam said sincerely. Elena reached up and ran her fingers through his curly blonde hair. He always looked as though he was up to no good, but she could tell that he meant every word. " I love you too, " Elena answered. " It was over you, you know.." Sam continued as he went back to pounding her pussy. Elena didn't know what he was talking about. "What do you mean?" "The day I came back with the bloody nose. Anissa had punched me because I told her that I didn't think I could resist you any longer."

Sam flipped Elena over and looked deeply into her eyes. His cock was as hard as a boulder inside her tight pussy. "Do you remember when you said my eyes looked like coffee beans?" Elena asked. Beads of sweat dripped down Sam's forehead as he continued to pump into his beautiful girlfriend. "Yes, I remember. God, you're so hot," Sam moaned as he lost himself in the depths of her womanhood.

Elena leaned forward and kissed Sam deeply on the lips. "Thank you," she said. Sam paused for a moment. "What are you thanking me for?" he asked. "Thank you for loving me..." she said, "and also, thank you for not being a serial killer, because I was pretty worried about that for a while."

The two lovers burst into a fit of laughter. Even though their countries and native ways of life were so far apart- their hearts were exactly where they wanted to be—together.

SEXUAL CHESS

KELLY SPACER

Chapter 1

Alana scanned the room with tired eyes. She always had difficulty sleeping the night before a tournament, and last night had been no different. She'd tossed and turned all night, and then there was a weird dream in which her dead mother was riding a cow with skin that looked like a chessboard. Tournaments always played games with her head.

Alana had a habit of bringing her queen out too early and was still chiding herself over last month's fiasco. It should have been a simple win—the other player had been rated lower than she was, and both she and her father had reviewed his track record. He was the kind of chess player who often leveraged cheap tricks, but who couldn't really think far enough ahead in order to win the game. He almost always used the same traps, castling and then slaughtering all the pieces in his way in a diagonal pattern, leading with his bishop. Nevertheless, it had been a bloodbath.

After her opponent had castled, he'd brought his bishop backward; she hadn't been prepared for that. Then, he'd started punching through her puny defenses, killing every one of her pieces in sight. First, a few pawns fell. Then, he'd taken her rook, and she was on the run. That was all it took. She was so frazzled that she couldn't see the board clearly. All she could hear was the tick tock of the chess clock, and her brain telling her just to make a move, *any move*. Alana panicked, and that was why she lost.

When her opponent announced, "checkmate" with a smirk, the room had erupted in cheers, and he'd been lifted up onto his father's shoulders and triumphantly carried around the room. That year, most of the tournament's players had been from India and simply did not want a female to win. She'd lost the competition not just for herself, but also for female players all over the world. So many of them had been rooting for her.

After the crushing loss, Alana had only lowered her head and shrunk away, not even bothering to collect her second-place trophy. Her father had chided her the entire way home.

"You embarrassed me today," he said through a veil of tears. " I did everything I could to prepare you. I just don't understand...why would you walk right into an obvious trap like that? I've made so many sacrifices to get you here... how could you do this to us, Alana? How could you do this to yourself?" Her dad wiped his tears away with the back of his hand.

Alana had cried silently the entire ride home.and all day the next day...and the day after that too. Eventually, weeks passed and with the exception of going to her classes—she'd managed to stay in bed the entire time.

She had to let that go now, though. She was eighteen now, and her new league was geared towards creating professional players. Things would happen that she couldn't anticipate—this was a part of the beauty of chess. If a move flustered her, she'd let the clock run. If she suspected that her opponent was laying a trap, she'd trust her instincts. She wouldn't make the same mistake twice.

Alana leaned back in her chair in the tournament hall, crossing one long leg over the other. Today, they were starting with speed rounds. She liked to refer to this part of the tournament as sudden death because it weeded out the weak players before the longer series that would be played tomorrow. In these speed games, she needed to watch out for little tricks—but if she didn't act impulsively or let herself be caught off-guard, she'd be just fine.

Alana ran an errant finger through her soft red hair and applied a thin coating of lip-gloss. It was time to get to business. Alana sat down at table A23 and waited for the line of opponents to file in. A bell rang, and the door opened. A bunch of teenagers flooded in, eager to win. Most of them were eighteen as she was—but there were a few ambitious ones that were much younger.

An Indian boy sat down at her table and smirked. He smelled of chutney and had the intelligent face of a doctor. He wasn't a good player, and Alana had the vague sense that she'd beaten him before—she'd beaten virtually all of them before. Alana made her first move and punched the clock, he countered and then clocked in. She captured his queen in fives moves, and then it was all over. "Check-mate!" Alana called and lifted her flag. An organizer came over and nodded. She extended her hand to the boy, as he got up and rushed away crying. "Next!" another organizer called.

The next guy who sat down was worse than the first. He reminded Alana of a person made entirely from marshmallows. His cheeks were puffy, and when it became obvious that he was going to lose, he just started moving pieces around the board haphazardly. Then he simply gave up and walked off, which gave her the win by default.

Now, it was break time.

The players filed into a room that had been set-up with some light banquet style fare. As soon as she was inside, her dad rushed over to her. Like the other parents, he'd been watching the live feed on the break room TV.

"You're doing good kid. I've got a feeling about this one...I really do..." he said, beaming. The other parents in the room flocked around their kids giving last minute tips and warnings. Alana caught the eye of a dark-haired young man across the room. He smiled slyly in her direction and winked at her, which made her uneasy. Who the hell did he think he was? Anyway, now wasn't the time to get distracted. She needed to focus. She could think about boys after she'd made the Harvard elite chess team. Nothing else was as important as making that team.

Alana sauntered over to the punch bowl and picked up a small plate from a nearby table as her stomach growled. She started to pile on cheese and crackers, nervously shoving some in her mouth at the same time. Her cheeks were filled to the brim with cookies when a smooth voice from behind her ran a few fingers through her hair. "I've read all about you," the voice said, "but the article didn't say you were so beautiful," he said as he touched her gently.

Alana spun around. She must have looked like a chipmunk storing food for the winter, because the seriousness in his voice broke when he saw her face; he burst into laughter. "Food hoarder?" he asked. "Or are you just part squirrel..storing up for the winter?" He laughed, looking down at her plate. "I think they have treatment centers for that." He smiled, crossing his arms. " No...I..um...I..." she couldn't find the words, or even manage to say anything through the enormous ball of food in her mouth.

"They tell me that you almost won last year, but that you brought your queen out too early. I'm the same way...I love the queen. She has so many useful... functions. It's hard to resist the charms of a beautiful woman," the guy said, winking again, "especially one so capable." Alana felt her throat go dry and worried she wouldn't be able to swallow the ball of food already in her mouth. "Do you know what I like to do with my queen? If I can get her away from the other players, when she's naughty I take her between my fingers, and I slide her right..." the young man was interrupted by Alana's father.

"Get away from my daughter, you scum!" the old man said, gently grabbing Alana by the shoulder to lead her away. The young man's own father chimed in now. "Your stupid daughter shouldn't even be here Barry; she's such a weak player. She belongs back in the kiddie league—a waste of space." Barry turned around with rage in his eyes. His face had turned beet-red. "Spoken like the cheating jackass that you are." Her dad spat to the young man's father.

Then, all hell broke loose.

Alana's dad and Alexander's father slammed into each other. Ivan had tackled Barry from across the room, and they landed on the banquet table, sending the entire cheese display crashing noisily to the floor, as people screamed and clamored to get out of the way. Then, the two men rolled around mumbling expletives at one another, throwing punches that thudded softly. Neither of them seemed to be actually winning the fight. Old rivalries were common in the world of chess.

A few minutes later, Alana patted her dad on the shoulder and watched as Alexander did the same. They were outside in the rain now, since both of their parents had been kicked out and banned for the rest of the day. The youngsters would be allowed to continue in the tournament, but their parents were out. Alexander exchanged a few more words and then shook his dad's hand while Barry gave Alana a deep hug. "Just don't bring your queen out too early again honey. Please—no matter what you do.... God help us." Alana kissed her dad softly on the cheek. There were tears in Barry's eyes as Alana closed the door to the fire exit, leaving both of their parents outside in the rain.

She was surprised to find that Alexander was still standing in the stairwell, waiting for her. "Your skirt is wet," he said gently. "Oh, it's just from the bottle of ginger ale. When my dad bit your father's eyebrow it toppled over and splashed on it," she said wistfully. Alexander nodded and pulled his sweater off up over his head. He approached her slowly and then tied it around her tiny waist. "That will help you stay warm...since you're already soaking wet." He said. Alana felt her face redden.

Alana expected him to move away, but he didn't. Instead, his hands started to wander around her stomach, feeling the sleek curvature of her waist. The entire thing made her feel dizzy, and almost as if all the air had gone out of the room. "I don't want this falling off of you in the middle of the tournament," Alexander said, as he tightened the sweater around her waist a little more. His hands were so strong and muscular, and his body felt good against hers. Her yanked her hard so that she was right up against him. She could feel his chiseled core pressing against her. Something else was pushing against her too—something firm and rock-hard.

Alana stepped away. "I'm not that kind of girl," she said, looking away. Alexander advanced again and started to stroke her cheek, while he looked deeply into her eyes. "Then what kind of girl are you, Alana?" he asked. Time seemed to stand still as he moved in closer, his lips drawing nearer to her pink glistening mouth. How good it would feel to kiss her, to press her body up against the wall and take her—right there in the stairwell.

Just then, an organizer opened the door. "Five minutes!" he announced—not seeming to notice that the two were locked in an intimate embrace. Then, the pieces in his mind came together. "No fraternizing between opponents. It seems you have violated...," the organizer said. Before he could finish his sentence and kick them out, Alana stepped away. " So glad you got that eyelash out of my eye, it was driving me crazy." She said. "I had an eyelash stuck to my contact lens, so sweet of Alexander to help, don't you think?" she said to the organizer as she followed him out of the stairwell. There were no rules against *that*.

Alexander smiled sincerely. What a woman.

Chapter 2

The day droned on for hours. So much of chess was about endurance, and as Alana slaughtered player after player, she wondered about Alexander's endurance. He was certainly muscular and fit—with such a beautiful chiseled jawline. *I bet he could go all night,* she thought—and then pushed the thought from her mind.

He was so incredibly hot. Alana fanned herself absentmindedly. The idea of Alexander was making her burn-up. She thought back to the way he had so skillfully tied his sweater around her waist. What if he'd been pushing her panties to the side instead? What if he'd just taken her right there in the stairwell? Alana looked up at her opponent who was still lost in thought. Alexander wasn't like the rest of the chess players—he was confident. She thought back to the way his full lips curved when he pouted...and lastly, she remembered that fantastic hardened bulge in his pants. Her face reddened when she secretly wondered if she could manage to squeeze all of his huge manhood inside her body—if it ever progressed to that. She's never gone that far before.

Then, the fire alarm started to blare. "Shit," Alana said aloud.

All the players stood up in unison, ready to evacuate but not wanting to walk away from their tables and be disqualified. Alana wiped more sweat from her forehead. It wasn't just the thought of Alexander that was making her hot. There was a fire.

An organizer quickly jogged into the room. "Please evacuate in a calm and orderly fashion," he said. It was as though he'd lit a match in a powder keg. All the players sprinted for the door in unison, and in the utter chaos of it all, Alana was somehow knocked to the floor. She hit her head when she landed and looked up with blurry eyes. The chess clock teetered over her head for a millisecond and then plummeted downward, landing on her head with a terrible thud. Everything went black.

Chapter 3

When Alana woke up, she felt as though she was on some kind of animal, moving—maybe a mule. Perhaps, she was riding a horse; she loved horses. No, she'd been at the chess tournament. There weren't any mules there. Alana shook the thought from her head. It was difficult to think clearly. Her head was lying in someone's lap. He was smoothing her hair back from her face and crying down all over her cheeks.

Alana opened her blurry eyes. She couldn't see clearly, but whoever it was seemed to have dark hair and kind eyes. It must have been Alexander. Alexander was so lovely. It felt nice—the way he was pushing her hair back from her face, but why was he crying? "I had a conditional scholarship to Penn State, based on the condition that I make the penultimate round of this tournament. You took me out of the game, yet again. This is the sixth time we've met, and yet you never remember me." Then, there were lips on her own. No—this wasn't Alexander. She smelled the chutney on his breath and immediately knew that it was her Punjab Akwabi—the boy with the face of a doctor. Then, something heavy slammed down on her face and red clouded her vision. Alana's head rolled to the side. She was so sleepy now...so very sleepy.

Then, she heard a rush of footsteps and a second voice. "Get the hell away from her, you lunatic!" *That was Alexander.* While she was too weak to move, she could see their blurry shapes wrestling on the floor of the makeshift tournament hall. She could hear the force of Alexander's fists smacking the weak shape of Punjab around.

Punjab didn't cry. He was laughing like a maniac or some kind of evil genius. "We're going to burn in here together, Alexander. If I don't have a future, neither will you guys." Alexander grabbed Punjab by the collar and pulled him in as though he might deliver a fatal blow. Then, he disregarded the thought, pushed him out of the way, and ran for Alana.

When he reached her, he wrapped his arms around her and gathered her into his muscular biceps. Alana groaned as he lifted her effortlessly from the floor and held her close. Her face was pressed up against Alexander's body, and she could feel his rippled hard abs against her.

The tournament hall was very quickly going up in flames. Fire soared up the nearby beams and danced onto the ceiling, as pieces of paint peeled and fell away like the falling petals of thousands of black flowers. Black smoke billowed upward, and the room was as hot as a sauna.

Alana groaned. She wanted to stand up so that she could help Alexander find a way out. She wanted to thank him...she wanted to tell him that she had wanted to kiss him in the stairwell. Sadly, when she tried to speak the only sound that came out was a garbled one that sounded like a dying cat. She wasn't even making whole words—she was babbling. Yet, Alexander was with her every step of the way. "I know...I know...I'm going to get you out of here. Don't you worry." He said, soothing her.

The room was entirely filled with black smoke now, and they approached a nearby wooden door. Alexander gently lowered Alana to the floor and pushed the door. It wouldn't budge. He paused for a moment, as if in through, and then dropkicked the frame in the metal. The door flapped open, and cold fresh air whooshed into the tournament room. Alexander gathered her back up into his arms and carried her outside, where they were then immediately surrounded by scores of fighter fighters—who immediately placed an oxygen mask over her face. Her father rushed over and began to stroke her hand, with tears streaming down his face.

" Punjab started the fire. He's still in there." Alexander said, through short deep gasps of air.

Chapter 4

Alana sat in her hospital room, still in a minor state of shock. The news had captured the dramatic moment when Alexander had carried her out of the burning building, and they'd been playing it on repeat all afternoon. There was also a video loop of Punjab screaming and wailing as police carried him off in cuffs while he screamed obscenities and babbled about his college entrance exam. He'd most certainly snapped.

Alexander had looked so burly and in-control. As he'd carried her across the threshold, there was a minor rip in his shirt and his abs rippled, while his face was full of concern for her. He'd looked at her with such loving eyes.

Alana was surprised to learn that the chess tournament was going to continue. A wealthy benefactor had heard about the youngsters' plight and had purchased a block of hotel rooms at a nearby Hilton, and had generously rented two of their banquet rooms. The mysterious benefactor had also added to the cash award that the tournament winner would receive. The scholarship was now up to $200,000. The game would go on. The game of chess always went on—just like life did, and now everyone would be out for blood.

Alana blinked for a moment. She hadn't noticed that someone was sitting in the chair in the corner of her hospital room. Her father always seemed to hover, and she simply assumed that it was him. He was probably there to make certain she was able to recover in time to make it back to the tournament. He was probably sitting over there thumbing through his old chess playbooks, as usual. He was obsessed.

Tears welled in Alana's eyes. She loved chess—she loved everything about chess from the way the small, sturdy pieces fit into her hands to the biographies of great players like Bobby Fischer. She loved how chess was a metaphor for life—how you could plan for so many things, but how in the end winning was always about the perfect combination of both skill and luck. She liked how people came together to play chess, how it united players from all over the world...but she did not like what chess had done to her relationship with her father.

Chess had given them many opportunities to be together—but it had also taken the normalcy out of her life. When she'd wanted to try to join the soccer team at school, he'd forbidden that after finding out that the team practice schedule would conflict with her weekend chess games. Instead of attending to prom, Alana found herself studying playbooks and psychology books, hoping to better her ability to anticipate the moves of her opponents. When people saw her dad—they saw his dedication to her and admired it—but no one ever actually stopped long enough to realize that his obsession with chess had effectively robbed her of her childhood. No one understood. Well, no one except maybe Alexander.

The voice that rang out startled her. " I was waiting for you to wake up," Alexander said. He was sitting in the armchair in the corner and Alana was shocked. "I told your dad that I'd keep an eye on you while he went to the bathroom," Alexander smirked. There was a bit of soot on his forehead, a smudge beneath his eye, and a burn on his left hand.

Alexander looked down at his hand. "While you were unconscious, Punjab lobbed a piece of flaming wood at my head—nice guy," Alexander smiled sarcastically. A knot twisted in Alana's stomach. What on earth had driven that guy so insane? On top of that, how could Alexander be so nonchalant about the whole thing; they'd almost died.

"I'm glad you're okay," Alexander said. "The tournament starts again at 9 am tomorrow, and I wanted to make sure you'd be able to play." He finished. "Why?" Alana sighed. Alexander smiled and leaned forward. She could feel his hot breath on her face, and she was almost sure that he would kiss her this time. "I want to see if I can beat you," Alexander smiled. His words made her stomach turn over. "And if you can't, what are you going to do? Are you going to be like Punjab and try to burn the whole place to the ground?" Alana asked. "No," Alexander responded. "I'm going to take you to dinner."

With that, he stood slowly, kissed her on the forehead, and left the room. Alana noticed that her core was wet and pounding. Her body longed to take Alexander inside—to squeeze his biceps as he bucked around on top of her. If he wanted a wild ride, she could certainly give him that.

Chapter 5

Alana sat in the new makeshift tournament hall, ready to play. She and Alexander were similarly rated, and so it would be a while yet before they had to face off. In fact, rumor had it that both she and Alexander were leading—he was trailing only a few points behind her.

A young blonde man sat down at her table and drummed his fingers against the edge of his chair thoughtfully. He seemed more interested in Alana than in the game. The guy's eyes were drawn up almost like tiny slits, or crescent moons. Alana started the clock and moved her pawn forward two spaces. She was surprised when the young man didn't counter. "I know it probably seems to you like Alexander cares about you a lot, but it he doesn't." The guy said. Alana was caught off-guard.

The blonde finally moved his pawn; he simply countered what she'd done with hers. He reached up and scratched his chin. "He was just telling everyone in the breakroom that he'd disarmed you enough to be able to beat you at the tournament." The guy swallowed. Alana's stomach suddenly felt like it was doing flips. Alexander's feelings for her had seemed so real. She wondered if it was really true. Was Alexander just leveraging her feelings towards him so that he could win a chess game? Why should this stranger care about what happened to her?

As if he was almost reading her mind, he responded. "My name is Simeon, and the reason I care is because Alexander did the same thing to my sister two years ago in Australia. He pretended like he was falling in love with her, and then when they faced-off during the final match, he told her it was all a lie and that he wanted to break-up, right then and there. She was so frazzled and heartbroken that she just got up and walked away. Alexander won by default."

Alana thought back to the fight between her father and Alexander's dad. Her father had said that Alexander's family was known for their cheap tricks inside the world of chess. If there was one thing she knew about her dad—it was that he knew his chess.

Alana countered against Simeon and quickly boxed in his king. "Checkmate!" she called. An event organizer rushed over and checked her work. As Simeon got up from the table, he looked back over his shoulder. "Remember what I told you," he said. " Do not trust Alexander. He has only one interest in you—and that's to make sure you lose."

The day droned on, and other players came and went. Alana couldn't stop thinking about Alexander. Weirldy enough, she was also proud of herself—she hadn't allowed herself to fumble. While her stomach churned away and her heart seemed to clack around in her chest, she remained focused on her goal. No matter what happened—she was going to win this year.

Chapter 6

Alana dipped one toe into the jacuzzi. Their new hotel had descended into a bit of chaos, and the younger players were running around in the halls playing tag, screaming at the top of their lungs. She needed to clear her mind for a while. She needed to stop focusing on Alexander and get her mind back on the game.

Slowly, Alana submerged her body into the warm water. It was an incredible feeling, to be enclosed in the wet warmth all around her.

She leaned back and gently started to feel her neck. Her body was so tense. Alana ran her thin hands across the glassy surface of the water. No one else was in the Jacuzzi room, and she had the whole place to herself. She leaned back against a jet and enjoyed the feel of the pulsating water against her back. As she closed her eyes, her mind wandered to thoughts of Alexander's body.

She remembered the feel of his rippling abs against his body, as well as his strong biceps supporting her weight. She recalled the way that he'd kicked the door open to save their lives, his strong calf muscles bringing the entire structure crashing wide open. The thought made her ache with want.

Alana looked around, considering the gravity of what she was about to do. If she got caught, there would be no way she could come up with a convincing fake explanation. She might even get kicked out of the tournament for lewd conduct, the thought of which made her chuckle. Ever so slowly, she pulled her bikini bottom down. Then she brought the fabric up out of the water and hid the bathing suit piece under her towel, which sat right next to her. Then, she waded over to the other side of the Jacuzzi, leaned against the jet stream, and gently parted her legs.

The warm water felt amazing against her clitoris, and she moaned and shuddered with pleasure as the Jacuzzi brought incredible ecstasy to her pussy. Then, she started to rock against the jet stream in a slow steady rhythm. Moving to a rhythm made the sensation feel even better. Her pleasure was mounting, and Alana tried to resist the urge to touch herself as the stream of water brought her closer and closer to a climax.

Finally, she could resist no more. Alana brought her right hand down and started to finger her engorged clitoris. She was so hard and erect. She pumped against herself gently, with her eyes still closed—summoning images of Alexander's body. He was such a handsome man—so strong, so brave, and well-spoken. When she thought about his eyes, her body went over the edge. Alana's core exploded in a powerful orgasm. She sighed—trying to recover and opened her eyes. Alexander was standing there watching.

Alana could feel her face turning bright red. Then, her embarrassment boiled over to anger. "What is wrong with you?" She said, furious, while stepping out of the Jacuzzi.

When the cold air hit her pussy, she remembered that she'd taken her bikini bottom off. She doubled over, fumbling to cover herself up. Alexander chuckled and offered her his towel. When she snatched it out of his hand, his face became angry too. "What's your problem?" Alexander asked. "I came in here for the same reason you did. I rounded the corner, and you were over there propped up orgasming, and it was awkward. I didn't know what to say." His eyes were very sincere.

"I suppose you've probably never seen a girl orgasm before," Alana said—trying to sound mean and sarcastic. " Actually, I haven't," Alexander said so quietly that the sound of his voice immediately made Alana feel guilty. "You mean to tell me that you've never..." Alana started. " But you're the same age as me—you're eighteen!" Alana said. Alexander's face grew tense. "My dad is obsessed with chess, same as yours. No time for girls. I never even got to play little league."

For some reason—Alana couldn't figure out why—but a sense of need overtook her. Finally, here was a person that understood. Yet, Simeon's words echoed in the back of her mind.

"Am I just a part of the game?" She asked. Alexander's face twisted up—confused. "Are you pretending to like me so that I'll be easier for you to beat in the tournament?" She asked. Alexander's clear eyes cast a dark shadow for a second. He looked sad. " In Australia, there was a girl that was a fierce opponent. My dad said we needed to strategize, so I made her fall in love with me. Then, during our final face-off at the tournament, I broke up with her. I'm ashamed that I did that, and I would never do it again. It's a huge regret that I have. It certainly wasn't a shining moment for me."

Alana turned to go—the thought that he'd done something so despicable made her want to flee from him right then and there. She turned to flee, and he gently grabbed her elbow. His skin was warm and firm. Rage coursed through her veins as he pulled her in. Then, ever so gently, he kissed her.

Alana felt as though her very soul was melting into a puddle. "How I feel about you is not a game," Alexander said—his eyes serious. Then, his hands were wandering all over her body. He cupped her breasts in his large hands and pushed her up against the wall, where he lifted her up. He reached around, unfastened the clip on her swimming top, and smiled as it fell to the floor.

He was irresistible. Alana ran her fingers through his thick hair and reached downward to feel his muscular buttocks. She could feel his hardness through his swimming trunks. He was pushed right up against her. Without hesitation, she reached over and pulled his swimming shorts down.

Alexander's mighty shaft stood robust and erect, the mammoth head glistening with beads of pre-cum. Alana lowered herself from his grip on the wall and gently enclosed his manhood in the palm of her hand; then she slowly started to stroke him.

Alexander moaned in delight as he worked her shaft, stroking up from the base so that his foreskin glided right over the tip of his dick. When he thought he might die from pleasure, she finally lowered herself over him and took the tip of him into her mouth. Alana sucked gently at first as Alexander strained—trying not to cum. Then, she sucked him harder and harder—mercilessly, as she continued to pump his shaft.

He could take it no longer. Alexander started to thrust into the tight canal of her throat—filling her mouth up with his dick. Her red hair bobbed up and down on him, and his heart was full of love. He'd never seen a girl as beautiful as she was.

Gently, he pulled her away and laid her down gently on one of the reclining pool chairs. He climbed on top of her and kissed her, reveling in the taste of his cock upon her lips. "Chess is just a game," he said. "My love for you is real." Just then, he thrust his hardness inside of her.

Alana had never had sex before, and she cried out for a moment—even though she didn't want him to stop. His huge girth was excruciating inside the tight slick tunnel of her pussy. "Relax sweetheart," Alexander said as he stroked her hair. Then gently he began to rock her, and pleasure racked both of their bodies.

Neither of them had ever known any sensation of such pure bliss. Alana luxuriated in the feel of Alexander's body covering her own, as he moved faster and faster. The more he rocked her, the more her body opened to accommodate him. Finally, neither of them could take it anymore—Alexander spewed his manhood inside of her and Alana felt his hot release pooling into her core. She came in a flash, her muscles clenching down on him so hard that he grunted and bucked some more—his mouth wide open as he spilled into her again. When they finally came apart, the playful tension between them was gone.

Alexander sat down on the chair beside Alana and stroked her hair. "I never really wanted to play chess, you know," he said. " I just wanted to make my dad happy," Alexander sighed. Alana nodded. "It was that way for me too for a while. Somewhere along the way, though—I got confused, and I also got really good at chess. When you play me tomorrow—give it your all—and then, maybe we can go on a date?" Alexander smiled and kissed her passionately. "Game on," he said, beaming.

Chapter 7

Alexander and Alana sat across from each other. The match was heated. So far, in all respects, they were equals. Neither of them was in a good predicament, but if either of them made a mistake, that would even the playing field out a bit.

Alexander looked over at Alana. Her brow was furrowed, and she was lost in concentration. Then, he moved his queen forward two spaces—thinking that she would force her bishop to retreat. Instead, she launched an assault. She took his queen with her rook, and then in four moves, she had him cornered. "You did it. You beat me. Call checkmate." Alexander said, smiling. Alana extended her hand, offering him a draw. " We can both win," Alana said. Alexander looked down to the board and then back up to her. " As long as I have you—I've won," Alexander beamed.

Alana smiled and called, "Checkmate!" and the tournament organizers rang the bell. She'd finally done it. She'd finally won the tournament.

Her dad burst in through the double doors, screaming, and wrapped her up in a huge hug. Then, she turned to Alexander who kissed her deeply and then hoisted her up on his shoulders.

The other players filed in, cheering and shouting her name at the top of their lungs. Tears of joy streamed down her face as Alana cheered with the rest of them.

Now that the game was over, the rest of her life could finally begin.

PICTURE PERFECT

GILLIAN BLACK

Chapter 1

Linda sat up straight and puckered her lips as Christof snapped the camera in front of her face. "That's it...that's perfect. Give me more! Give me more, Linda." Linda growled and hooked her fingers into the tangled shape of a claw, then she pulled her lips back from her teeth and sneered a little, trying to look like a tiger. She looked mostly like an Amazonian woman but was sexy just the same. Her dark hair looked primal, lustrous, and magnificent. Her distinct features had made all the magazines in Philadelphia hail her as the second coming of Gia. Linda appreciated that comparison because Gia was her idol. When she'd wanted to start modeling, she'd intentionally sought out the very same photographers that Gia had once worked with, hoping that they could do the same for her and elevate her career to the status of Supermodel. As things currently stood, she was well on her way. At last count, there were three billboards in Times Square currently bearing her likeness, yet the money was a different matter. She'd signed a bad deal with her talent manager and saw less than sixty percent of her earnings. Still, next month, she'd be doing a Vogue cover shoot if all went as planned. Life was good.

The shutter on Christof's camera continued to click rapidly. He paused for a moment as a makeup artist applied a little more foundation to Linda's face. Christof fumbled with the camera a bit and slowly wiped his blonde hair back, looking much like a muscled surfer. He started to scan through some of the photographs on the camera's LED screen. "How are they?" Linda asked, expecting to hear him say that the photographs were fantastic. Christof looked up with tears in his eyes. "Your heart has been too hardened by the world, my love. I can see no vulnerability—just artifice. There is nothing here that I can use." Christof twirled a little locket that he wore around his neck and clicked his teeth decisively. He placed the tip of the locket into his mouth and sucked on it. On the necklace, there was a picture of a one-eyed Chinaman holding a bleeding heart.

Christof's words had been so calculated that it made her shudder. She walked over towards the sofa, catching a glimpse of herself in the mirror. She wanted to wash her makeup off so that he could see her real face, maybe that would help things. At that moment, she longed to somehow show Christof that she had depth, that she too had suffered pain and loss. Linda hated it when people assumed that she was vapid because of her chosen career. There was so much more to her than her looks.

"Your photos look so ugly. It's like there's all the beauty of you against the backdrop of someone with no personality. The only thing that comes through in these photos is falsehood. It makes me feel sick. Get your clothes on. I can't use you. I'll have to ask the agency to send someone else." Christof barked.

The door opened and a raven-haired man who was both tall and muscled sauntered in. His deep brown eyes scanned the room and stopped on Linda for a moment, then he smiled. "Antonio!" Christof cried with glee, as he rushed over and patted his friend on the back. "I didn't think you were going to be back from Uruguay for another month!" Antonio cleared his throat. Linda noticed the little ripple of his stubble. "The food we were delivering for the children was intercepted by thugs, so the company sent me back stateside because the insurance company was concerned about some liability issues. Ever since my collection was accepted by the Whitney, they're afraid that insurgents might try and kidnap me to hold me hostage for ransom. So, basically, my success was ironically the very thing that separated me from my dream job." There was genuine sadness in his voice. "I miss her so much Christof...too much." Antonio's voice trailed off.

The two men looked up as if they suddenly remembered that someone else was in the room. Linda stood slowly and extended a warm hand in Antonio's direction. "I'm pleased to meet you," she said. He gave her a half smile and bent to kiss the top of her hand with his silky warm Italian lips. "I hope that Christof hasn't been torturing you," he gave her a sly smile. Linda looked down, not wanting to explain that she'd just been fired, more or less. "Her eyes are so beautiful, Christof," Antonio said. "I bet you were able to get some amazing photos of her." He smiled and then stopped when we realized the tension in the room. As if he understood, Antonio patted Christof on the back again. "You have a great subject here, but you're working too hard. You look tired. Let's just all try and get a drink. You can come back to this when you feel more relaxed."

A few hours later, somehow the three of them found themselves at a dive bar taking shots of tequila. Christof didn't seem happy that Linda was coming along, but he was tolerating her presence. Linda was secretly hoping that she'd be able to somehow get back on Christof's good side. Despite her success, she was unbelievably low on cash. She needed the job to work out.

"So tell me, Linda. What is your passion?" Antonio asked. Linda swallowed. "Modeling," she said without hesitation. "So basically, your passion is to show yourself off to the rest of the world and to be admired," Christof spat snidely, obviously drunk. "Do you know how many other people share that dream?" Christof asked. "It's common nowadays to want fame, but to have no skills that are worthy of it." He said snidely.

Antonio draped his arm protectively around Linda's shoulder and drew her nearer. The warmth of his body felt good. She could smell a slight trace of his shampoo and swooned a little. Antonio repeated his question, "Tell me about your passion, Linda. I want to hear what you have to say, ignore this animal."

Linda swallowed. "Modeling isn't about ego..in fact, it's just the opposite," Linda said softly. Christof laughed loudly, then abruptly quieted, smacked the table and pointed at her "you're delusional." He said, cracking up. "Wait...wait, let's hear her out," Antonio repeated. "Give Linda a chance to speak," he said to his friend. Linda swallowed again.

Linda fingered at a napkin on their table and then looked up. "When you're a model, you become a living work of art. Sometimes the photographer wants you to stand out, but other times, your job is to blend in with things—the scenery, your clothing, the very job of a good model is to make yourself less visible, and to in many ways become less of a person. I let artists use my body as a canvas. I put aside what I think and what I want and what I feel.. all in the service of art. That's why I love modeling so much."Christof paused a long while and then exploded into laughter again. " And what of your ego? You talk about modeling like it's some kind of religion, but you're a part of advertising, young lady. You're used to manipulate people into spending their money. So, regardless of if you're some kind of sanctimonious bitch, the fact remains that your face is flat and you destroy the morale of virtually every photographer that has the misfortune of working with you. You are legitimately talentless. And also brainless, it appears." Christof sneered. " Christof!" Antonio gasped. "You shouldn't talk to people like that." He chided. "That girl's a talentless whore," Christof said, leaning over and almost falling to the floor, drunk.

Linda grabbed her purse as tears swelled up in her eyes. "This is why you don't see vulnerability in my eyes, Christolf—it's because you're a jerk. You have difficulty finding depth in my photos because there is so little depth in you. And your career was in ruins long before I came along." And with that, she slid out of the booth, threw a little money down on the table to pay for her drink, and walked off in tears.

Chapter 2

When Linda had made her dramatic exit, she hadn't accounted for the possibility that she might have difficulty in hailing a taxi. For more than twenty minutes, she stood at the curb with her arm in the air, clutching her purse. The taxis seemed to favor the surrounding businessmen clad in expensive Brooks Brothers and Armani suits to the damsel who was so clearly in distress. Their shiny shoes reeked of money, of the assurance of a good tip. With tears streaming down her face, between sobs, and with black mascara running down her cheeks, she probably didn't look like very much of a safe bet. Linda sighed. Worse come to worst, she could always take the subway. After all, even though she was beautiful, she wasn't some kind of helpless woman that couldn't manage to come to her own aid. She could take care of herself.

Linda thought back to the way in which Christof had called her vapid and her stomach turned over. He had no idea what he was talking about, obviously, he was projecting—but his harsh words still hung in the air. Linda hadn't always been beautiful. She'd passed through her teenage years awkwardly, and both of the crushes that she'd had during that time had gone up in flames. First, there had been her best friend Elise, with whom she'd attended grade school and later college.

Linda and Elise had grown up together in the same town. As kids, they often had sleepovers, where they stayed up giggling until the wee hours of the morning. As they grew together, Elise became more and more desirable to Linda—until one night she could take it no more. After a few drinks Linda professed her undying love for her friend, and sadly, it didn't go well. Linda leaned in to kiss Elise beneath the comforter in their shared college dorm room and Elish had slapped her hard across the face. Then, to make matters worse—Elise had gone to their Resident's Assistant with the entire story, requesting to be moved to a new room. Soon after, the entire dorm was abuzz with exaggerated versions of what had happened. No one would agree to be Linda's roommate for fear of being subjected to unwanted sexual advances, and so she was eventually moved to a private suite at the end of the hall as if she'd been placed in quarantine. Her new room looked like a makeshift closet and had no windows. When her parents had come to visit later in the year, she hadn't had the courage to tell them the real story of why she was living in something that looked like an attic.

Linda had met her first boyfriend and first love Barkley, as a result of that fiasco. A few girls had cruelly painted the word "Lesbo" onto the hood of her car. Barkley worked at a neighborhood paint store and had done all he could to help her remove the words from her car. In the store parking-lot, they'd covered washcloths in paint remover and he'd helped her try to gently get the word off of her vehicle.

A few hours later they'd found themselves panting, as their hands nervously wandered all over each other's bodies while they lay together, twisted up in the back seat of her car, breathing heavily.

In a weird way, Antonio had reminded her a little bit of Barkley, except for the fact that Barkley had always been protective of her and had behaved like a gentleman. Christof was clearly a brute—and only a man with some serious character deficits would decide that he was Christof was friend material.

Linda reached up into the air again, having worked herself up. "Taxi!" She yelled at the top of her lungs while waving a hand in the air. A few more yellow cabs zoomed by. Why wouldn't any of these taxi drivers stop for her? "Hey!" she yelled, as yet another taxi sped by, and pulled over on the side of the curb to pick up a handsome man wearing a suit. Finally, a shabby looking taxi with a dent on its front bumper scuddled to a stop right in front of her. A plume of exhaust squirted out of its tailpipe.

As Linda wrapped her hand around the handle and prepared to get in, an older gentleman jumped into the backseat. She could feel that her face was burning with rage. Did anyone this town have any class? Did anyone in this town have any respect? What about manners...just basic manners? Was this man really trying to steal her cab in a rainstorm? Had humanity really come to that?

She was ready to slam the door when the older man smiled at her and made a come-hither motion with his fingers. "Come in from the rain, sweetheart. You are Linda, no?" Despite her better judgment, Linda slid into the backseat of the cab with him. The older gentleman handed the driver a wad of cash. "Please take this lady wherever she wants to go first, and then you can take me to Flower Street." The driver counted the wad of cash and tried to hand a few bills back to the older man. "Keep it, friend." He said. Linda looked over at the man and then gave the driver her address. He turned up the heat as they started off.

"Forgive my son," the man started. She recognized his accent—it was similar to that of Antonio. "I arrived shortly after you left and he asked me to see you home, while he puts his dog of a friend into a cab." Linda's mouth flopped open. So, Antonio did have some decency in him, after all. "I was supposed to be coming by to drop these off." The older man patted his briefcase. "What are they?" Linda asked. The man's face grew grim. "Blueprints, a deed...ghosts of a past life. Antonio hasn't been able to find a landlady, you see..." the older man said. Linda furrowed her brow. "My son owns a home about 40 minutes from here. He bought the property a few years ago because he'd intended to turn the house into individual apartment units. He needs a landlady because as a photographer, he travels frequently. Sadly, the last lady accidentally set herself on fire and we can find no replacement." Linda swallowed. Perhaps overtaken by a moment of utter madness, "I'll do it." She said without hesitation.

Chapter 3

When Linda arrived, she was totally blown away. She'd expected some kind of dilapidated house, but Antonio's estate was more like a castle. There were a few traces of the fire in the kitchen. The ceiling in there was scorched, as well as some of the floorboards, but as aside from that, nothing was in disarray. She pulled her luggage behind her as she started to explore the mysterious mansion. She knew that Antonio was talented, but had no idea that he only worked by choice. He'd inherited millions from his family's estate. She wondered about him. His father had said that Antonio would be also living at the estate in between his faraway photography assignments. It would be Linda's job to make sure that all the repairs went smoothly.

She'd seen the inside of Antonio's studio a few times during her tour of the property. It seemed that regardless of where he was in the world, he managed to take close-up shots of redheaded women. He'd taken a stunning nude photograph of a woman in Paris who's sat staring at him cross-legged with a cigarette propped between her full lips, her red hair lustrous and full, as it covered her shoulders. There was a similar photo that Antonio had taken in Ireland of a woman tending to a dilapidated rowboat. Her red spirals of hair looked wild, and framed her face as she grinned mysteriously into the camera. All of the women had red hair. Antonio seemed to be attempting to try and recreate something or someone.

Most of everything inside the massive home was covered in dust, and Linda headed up the massive staircase to try and find a bedroom. Her suitcase thunked loudly against the wood as she pulled it up the stairs. Finally, when she reached the top of the stairwell, she'd reached the beginning of two long corridors. The one to the left looked dark and foreboding and so she decided to traverse the nearer one to her right. As she slowly started to head down the hall, she could hear a distant scratching sound. Linda stopped, hoping there weren't squatters hidden inside the building—she'd never thought of that.

She'd seen plenty of documentaries on homeless people who squatted inside abandoned buildings. Maybe they'd thought that the estate had been vacated, and had perhaps moved in.

Linda let go of her suitcase handle and pressed her body up against the wall. Thinking quickly, she grabbed a nearby vintage candelabra. If someone tried to attack her, she could thunk them over the head with the candlestick. It was heavy enough to kill. She held her breath as she crept towards the scratching sound, her eyes darting back and forth. " I'm not going to hurt you. I just need you to vacate the property." Linda called. "The police are on the way, but if you come out now, I'll let you go and I won't press any charges, you have my word." Of course, the police weren't actually coming. Linda hadn't even dialed them, but the squatters didn't need to know that. She reached a huge pink bedroom at the end of the hall. The scratching was coming out of a closet in there." Linda's heart was throbbing in her chest, clacking rapidly like a runaway train. Adrenaline pumped through her body and her body was ready for fight or flight. Linda yanked the closet door open and something furry and black lunged out, wrapped its arms around her face. Linda screamed in horror, as the body blinded her view. It was a cat. Linda slammed to the ground and the cat hurried off, obviously, it was just as terrified as she was.

She sat up and sighed deeply as she rubbed her head. What a perfect start.

Later that evening, Linda fumbled around in the partially destroyed kitchen. She'd brought a few soup cans with her, but hadn't been prepared for the level of devastation within this area of the house. When she turned the faucet to release some water, there was a deep metallic groaning. The wall seemed to sputter and black slime oozed out of the hole. Linda sat down at the table, feeling defeated.

Just then, the front door slammed. It was Antonio. He smiled as she slowly trod into the kitchen with a large bag in one arm, filled to the brim with Chinese food. "I had a feeling you might need something to eat," he said to her. Linda chuckled, standing up, to take the bag of food from him. Together, they unpacked their meal and then sat down. Wordlessly, they both filled their mouths with noodles. Finally, they both paused to get a little air.

" I just got back from the base of Mount Fuji," Antonio said with a sly grin. He pulled his camera out of his backpack and started to flip through some photos on its LED screen. Linda couldn't help but notice how beautiful he looked in that moment. His thick but well -shaped eyebrows were furrowed in concentration as he scanned through his pictures, trying to find the right one. His brown eyelashes were incredibly thick, and his features were both chiseled and thoughtful. He was beautiful to look like and reminded Linda of some renderings she's seen of the archangel Gabriel. "I've always wanted to go to Mt.Fuji" Linda added, genuinely impressed. "I've been trying to get there for a long time, but had a lot of difficulties getting a press pass, so that I could photograph these areas." He handed Linda the camera and she scanned the photo display forward. First, there was a photo of yet another redhead—an Asian lady with red hair, with was quite beautiful. Then, there was a photograph of a corpse with its mouth gaped open, and it's eyes glazed over, and a few worms wriggling around where the man's tongue should have been. Linda almost dropped the camera as she clasped her hand over her mouth and turned away, trying to clear her mind of the horror she'd just seen. Antonio gently took her hand across the table. For a moment, they shared a knowing glance. "I know you've suffered loss too," he said in a whisper. "Who did you lose?" He asked softly. "My mother," Linda answered solemnly.

Chapter 4

Later that night, Linda tossed and turned. She dreamt of Antonio's muscled body, shirtless and strong. He ran his large fingers down her face and gently kissed the back of her hand. His beautiful fingertips wandered around to the back of her body, where he massaged her in rhythmic motions, and then reached up—his touch lingering at one of her nipples. "Antonio," Linda said, embarrassed. " I know you feel for me what I feel for you," he said. The sadness in his eyes was almost palpable.

"Come to me," he'd said as he wore a billowing white shirt. In the dream, he'd taken her hand and led her to a cellar door. "I keep all my secrets locked up in here." He said. As Linda had descended the basement steps, she was surprised to find herself down there... some alternate version of herself. Though, instead of black hair—her doppelganger had red hair. Linda's twin blinked at her kindly. There was something child-like in the way the other Linda looked. She sniffed the air and then smiled widely, revealing a bloody mouth that had no teeth in it. Then, the other Linda let her jaw drop open and she released a scream that could have woke up the dead. "Get out of my house!" the woman screamed. "Get out, or you will burn! You will burn! Stay away from my husband!"

Linda woke up, sitting straight up in her bedroom covered in sweat. She wiped some of the wetness away with the back of her hand and stifled a whimper. Then, she noticed it... the entire room was filled with thick billowing smoke.

Linda dropped to her hands and knees and crawled over to the door, feeling the door handle tentatively. It was a little warm, but it wasn't hot. She opened the door and was horrified by what she found on the other side. The ceiling in the hallway was covered in flames and the fire was quickly spreading. " Antonio!" Linda screamed. The smoke was black and thick and she could hardly breathe! On her hands and knees, she crawled over to Antonio's room and pushed the door open. He was laying on the bed, his eyelids clamped shut. "Antonio, wake up! Antonio, the house is on fire!" Linda screamed. She grabbed him by his undershirt, attempting to pull him out of the burning room. His eyes shot open. He grabbed her hand firmly around her wrist. Just like that, all the flames vanished and faded away. Linda felt as though she might vomit.

"What is going on?" Antonio demanded. Linda looked around, trembling. "The house...the house was on fire and I was trying to save you!" She screamed, tears streaming down her face. "The house was on fire!" she repeated. Antonio stood, then bent down and scooped her up into his strong arms. "Nothing is on fire here, darling. The fire was a long time ago and it has long since been put out. Let me put you to bed." A momentary sense of rage flew through her body, and for no reason at all, Linda began to flail about, punching wildly.

Antonio carried her as though she was weightless. Just the sensation of his touch brought her incredible comfort. Before she knew it, he was laying her back down in her bed, pinning her down with his muscled arms. She breathed a sigh of relief.

The flames on the ceiling were gone. The suffocating black smoke was gone. Everything was right in the world. Antonio reached down to smooth the hair on her head, and without thinking, Linda reached up and drew him in. Her full lips pressed against his, and before she knew what had happened she was pulling his shirt up and over his head and throwing it carelessly into the corner. Obviously, they'd both had pent up frustrations that were now coming to light. Antonio reached around and tore her nightgown, splitting the fabric in two, with very little effort. Now the were both naked. As he climbed on top of her, she reached around to squeeze his muscular ass. Antonio groaned as he decorated her silky skin with kisses, making his way up from her collarbone. Then, he opened his mouth and took in the tip of her nipple. He sucked gently and rhythmically as he pulled her in at the waist. Linda was overcome with desire.

Her core was soaking wet as her body opened itself to him—hoping for penetration, hoping that he would soon drive himself inside of her to fulfil her deepest desires. Antonio continued to kiss her all over, running his fingers all over her soft skin. He lapped at her nipple and she could feel the hardness of him against her thigh. Linda looked down, Antonio's cock was hard and erect, his tip glistening with pre-cum. She pushed him over on his back and descended upon him, taking his massive shaft down into the depths of her throat. She sucked him hard, enjoying the faint groaning sounds that he made as he gently bucked his hips, urging her to take more of him inside. Linda licked her lips, enjoying the wonderful salty taste of his precum. Her pussy throbbed with need. She took him further down her throat, so much so that she gagged, when her lips reached his balls. He was in her up to the hilt. "Holy fuck," Antonio gagged.

Then, Linda quickly withdrew and climbed up onto his lap. She made deep eye contact as she slowly guided his huge shaft into the depths of her womanhood. Antonio gasped as he descended into the impossibly tight canal her body. She was soft, wet, and unbelievably tight. Linda began to rock back and forth. Her pleasure mounted with every motion—she simply couldn't help herself. She bounced up and down on his shaft as he lay there groaning until her pleasure began to mount. He felt so good. She arched her back and swayed her hips while she rode so that she could take more of his magnificent shaft inside her body. Then, as the pleasure reached an unbelievable high she bounced up and down, enjoying the feel of his cock ramming into up against her g-spot. He was in her so deep. The pleasure had reached a fever pitch, and Linda could think of nothing but of cumming. She rode Antonio faster and harder until her juices began to spew, followed quickly by his fantastic release. Soon after, they lay together in bed as he stroked her hair gently.

"When I first met you, I wished that your hair was red, but I've come to love your brunette locks," he said. Then he swallowed and his eyes grew serious.

"I don't want you to leave me," Antonio said softly. Linda smiled. "What makes you think I'd ever want to leave." A moment of silence passed between them, then the light flickered on overhead. With a loud smack, it shattered and sprayed pieces of glass throughout the room. Both Linda and Antonio jumped up from the bed. "Was it a power surge?" Linda asked, as she pulled on one of Antonio's oversized T-shirts. He shook his head.

"It's my wife."

Chapter 5

When Linda had heard the word "wife" she went into a blind rage. "You're married!" She howled. "Why didn't you tell me you were married?" Linda demanded. Antonio combed a few fingers through his scalp, tears welling up in his eyes. "What kind of shit show are you running here? You bring girls in here for some kind of sick revenge? Is that what you do?" Linda wanted to know. Antonio cleared his throat. "My wife is dead, Linda. Her spirit is trapped here. Sometimes she appears as fire, and other times as a black cat."

"My wife suffered from terrible depression. One night, after a fight, she climbed into the river and she drowned herself. Her body was never recovered, but the cadaver dogs did find her nightgown on a rock. My wife is a ghost. She's alive as a ghost now."

Linda stood back and swallowed. She cocked her head to the side, "You've gone mad. Something has made you insane," she said, mostly to herself, ready to storm out of the room. Just then, a wall of flames erupted from the floor. She flew back.

"Stop it, Angel! Stop this at once!" Antonio called into the air. Immediately, the flames died down. He looked over the Linda and helped her up from the floor. "I had hoped to make this place into apartments or maybe some kind of Bed and Breakfast but my love's spirit is angry. She attacks every woman that sets foot in this place."

Linda wanted to doubt him, but she had seen the ghostly flames twice now. "What happened to the woman who worked here...before I came," Linda asked. "She was making dinner in the kitchen one night and my wife...my dead wife set her hair on fire. She ran throughout the room trying to put the fire out, and eventually found her way out into the front yard, which is why the floorboards are burned there. When she got outside, she died of shock." Linda squinted in disbelief.

"I've tried everything. I've tried priests and priestesses and psychics and medicine men and no one can get her to move into the light. I had hoped that maybe Angel would take a liking to you. She was a photographer like me, you see. Before that she'd been a bit of a model, though not the model you are."

Linda felt as though she was totally overwhelmed with emotion. She wasn't crazy—the flames had been some kind of eery manifestation. She wanted to flee from the house and go somewhere else, but the fact remained that she had no money—no money at all.

"Please forgive me," Antonio pleaded. "I made certain that the kitchen stayed out of order for your safety. You see, she generally only uses fire. It's how she communicates, I think." Linda felt as though her head was spinning. She'd been living with a ghost. All this time, Antonio's wife had been under her nose.

Just then, there was a gruff knock at the door. Before Antonio moved to answer it, Linda saw the shape of a woman pass through one of the other door frames. She'd simply darted by on her tiptoes. Her hair was long and red, like the women Antonio photographed.

When Antonio went to answer the door, Linda followed Angel's ghostly shape in the other direction. "Come on," Angel's ghostly voice called to her. Linda followed the ghost on her tiptoes. They crept out the back, down further and further into the massive garden. The ghost led her behind shrubs to a swing. Two sets of initials were carved into the seat. "Follow me, " the ghost whispered again, as she dashed further back into the garden. Linda had to struggle to keep up. The ghost laughed as she went, and her beautiful flowing red hair rippled through the air. Finally, the ghost settled on a little plot of land and pointed downward. She placed one finger to her lips as if to silence, Linda. "Chinaman," Angel the ghost whispered, before vanishing into thin air.

Chapter 6

Linda knew exactly what Angel had wanted her to do, and she did it without hesitation. She grabbed a shovel from inside the gardener's shed and had started to dig. Deeper and deeper, Linda cleared the earth away, until finally, her shovel thudded against something solid. There was some kind of chest in there.

Linda pushed away the dirt with the palms of her hands and then slowly opened the huge box and drew back, gagging. There was a woman inside, who was half decomposed. Her face was twisted up in a mask of horror and her beautiful red hair was matted with mud. Linda noticed that one of the fingernails on her left hand was missing. Antonio was a murderer. Antonio had killed his wife and he would surely kill her too if he found out that she knew. Linda shut the lid of the makeshift casket and slowly backed away. They had some kind of company right now. Perhaps she could sneak upstairs and dial the police while Antonio was distracted with the guest.

As soon as Linda crossed the threshold to the house, the ring of familiar laughter filled her ears. It was Christof. Even though she'd tried to shut the door quietly, the old door had given her away. "Come in here," Antonio smiled at her. "Oh god, I didn't know you were still dragging this ugly hag around." Christof sneered. "Stop that," Antonio demanded in a harsh voice. "I want you to learn to be civil," Antonio added to his friend. "Why should I be civil? You know as much as I do that Linda's not going to amount to anything," Christof said dismissively. It was as if a match had been lit. "In my home, you will not treat anybody with disrespect," Antonio said. "Your home, brother?" Christof sneered. " Our mother left this home to you because you tricked her! I was the rightful heir to her fortune! I was the one who should have inherited this place, not you!" The pieces began to come together in Linda's mind. Christof and Antonio were half-brothers.

Christof raised a fist and swung at Antonio who jumped out of the way. Then, Christof lunged again, this time locking his brother into some kind of hold. Christof bit Antonio hard on the neck, ripping away flesh, and he flailed around screaming, grabbing for anything…anything to get him to stop. Somehow, Antonio's hands tore away the locket that Christof always seemed to wear around his neck. Antonio ripped the locket off and it clattered to the floor where it lay open. Inside the locket, there was one whole fingernail, which was painted and decorated with a blue flower. Linda could tell that immediately, Antonio knew what it was. Rage filled his features.

Linda had gotten it all wrong. Antonio hadn't murdered his wife—Christof did.

Christof brought his face up and grinned. "You never even suspected me, did you? That suicide note I wrote in her handwriting about going to drown in the river...it was a masterpiece. You should have seen her face. You should have seen the fire in your wife's eyes as I choked her to death." Antonio jumped up and flung his entire body at Christof knocking him to the floor, where he lay there laughing like a maniac. Antonio punched his face over and over again, but still, Christof just lay there on the floor laughing. Then, his expression turned icy. "Revenge is a dish best served cold, brother. You might have gotten all the money in the family, but ultimately, I got the thing that really mattered. I took your happiness." Christof said as he flipped Antonio over and smashed his head hard on the floor. Then, he looked up at Linda and sprinted after her as though he was some kind of vicious animal.

Linda wasn't very fast, but she was smart. She ran through the back door out into the yard with Christof at her heels. She zigged and zagged through the hedges and shrubs, back to the place where she'd left her digging shovel. Christof's voice was loud behind her. " Here kitty kitty kitty," he said. When he noticed the dug-up makeshift casket he leaned down to examine it, and Linda whacked him over the head. *Thunk.*

Everything went black.

Chapter 7

The police had been quick to arrive. The case was one that was easy to piece together. Christof's DNA was all over Angel's corpse, as well as all over the fingernail he'd worn inside the locket. Yet, there was one more thing.

Linda closed her eyes and placed her palm over her heart. An image of the fire came to her one last time. When she closed her eyes, she could see Angel dancing near the fire pit in the yard. Linda rushed out to the fire pit. One of the stones in the ground was loose. She pulled it back to reveal a small metal box. Inside the box there were a few documents that it seemed Angel had hidden intentionally. At the very center, there was a picture of she and Antonio at their wedding, standing in front of a blazing fire pit, as they exchanged vows. There was a note on the back, which read, "As your wife, I vow to always love you, but also to do my best in protecting you. You are not only my lover, but also my best friend." Angel hadn't been trying to frighten or torture any of those women; she'd been trying to warn them.

When Antonio read Angel's words, he collapsed into a heaping pile of sobs into Linda's arms. Linda gently reached down and kissed him on the lips, as she watched Angel's ghost slowly drift out of sight.